Other books by William Post

The Mystery of Table Mountain

The Miracle

A Call to Duty

Gold Fever

The Blue Ridge

A Doctor by War

Inner Circles

The Evolution of Nora

Darlene

The Tides of War

The First Crossing of America

The Gray Fox

Captain My Captain

Alaskan Paranormal

Some Boys from Texas

The Law and Alan Taylor

A New Eden

Kelly Andrews

Lost in Indian Country

A Trip to California

Lost in the Ukraine

A Ghost Tribe

The Wrong Place

Pure Love

A Promise to a Friend

Sid Porter

Gathering of a Family

A Stranger to Himself

Hard Times

The Riflemen

A Soldier and a Sailor

A GHOST TRIBE

WILLIAM POST

authorHOUSE®

AuthorHouse™
1663 Liberty Drive
Bloomington, IN 47403
www.authorhouse.com
Phone: 1 (800) 839-8640

Published by AuthorHouse 07/11/2017

ISBN: 978-1-5246-9915-4 (sc)
ISBN: 978-1-5246-9914-7 (e)

Print information available on the last page.

PREFACE

This book is about love. Many different kinds of love. It starts with tragedy, and then moves on to a friendship between a middleaged Indian and a thirteen year old boy. The boy has lost his family and the Indian his tribe.

As they travel they decide to form their own tribe. They call it the *Ghost Tribe*. Other members come into the tribe, when they aid others in overcoming tragedy. Both the Indian and the boy have a deep belief in God. That is the basis of all love.

Jesus has promised each of us, that if we will invite him into our hearts, he will abide in us with his Holy Spirit. I can promise you, the reader, if you have not done this, you should, because you will be much happier. The love of Jesus passes all understanding. It inundates you, and you are never alone.

Being forgiven of your sins is like taking a huge load off your back. Will you sin again? Of course, but each year you will leave some of that garbage behind, and live a fuller and more productive life.

When Christ returns, he will give us, as he promised, a glorified body like the one he had after he was resurrected. I think the greatest part of having a glorified body is that you will never sin again, as sin is not allowed into Heaven.

I still remember as an a ten year old boy, receiving Christ in an old wooden tabernacle in Roscoe, Texas. God penetrated my heart that night and I inherited everylasting life. But the best part, was that I had someone with me for the rest of my life.

Although not a religious book, it speaks of the inner feelings of people. You will identify with some of the characters and their actions. I hope you enjoy it.

LIST OF CHARACTERS

Ben Carson - Lee

Chief Lee - Doctor Lee - Lesta Katonka - Paul Lee

Cary Elder - Lee - Dobbs

Milton Evers - A salesman who bought Cary at age fourteen

Mr. Baker - A man who bought Cary then threw her out

Captain Robert Ward - Lee

Homer Dobbs - owner of a way station

Alta Dobbs - wife

Hank Dobbs - son

Barney Dobbs - son

Sarah Ward nee Dobbs

Doctor Samuels - alcoholic doctor

Hiram Welder - original owner of the mine west of Verdi

Carl Elder - father of Cary

Nelda Elder - wife

Debbie Elder - daughter, later wife of Barney Dobbs

Otis B. Odom - owner of the ranch south of the Elder - Welder ranch

Bob - Odom's foreman

Bill and Steve - Odom's ranch hands

Eduardo Nunez - foreman of Elder/Welder ranch

Maria Nunez - wife of Rudi

Rudi Nunez - brother of Eduardo

Juanita Nunez - wife of Eduardo

Cole Byers - contractor

Mildred Byers - wife of Cole - partner of Cary

Chester Martin - Mayor of Verdi

Greta - waitress of Cary's donut shop

Winston Hampton - CEO of the Lee's businesses

Rae Ling Hampton - wife of Winston

Martin Landry - alcoholic lawyer and later lawyer of the Lee Corporation

Abel Collins - gunman at Verdi

Brown brothers who were hanged for killing Jack Kilgore

Roscoe Evers - sheriff of Verdi

Bob Hanigan - Missionary

Ellen, Daphne and Marsha - missionaries

Colonel Clemens - officer in charge of the fort

Bill Brown - Indian agent in Cheyenne

Amy Mason - first wife of Ben Lee

Lon and Lara Mason - parents of Amy

Lloyd - partner of Amy's first husband

Roger - Amy's first husband

CONTENTS

Chapter 1

SLAUGHTER OF A WAGON TRAIN

It was the summer of 1865. The Civil War was over. Ben Carson's father was speaking to his family. He said, "Our way of life is over here in Virginia. For that matter, the whole South's way of life has ended. They will move their army here to cram their way of life down our throats. I feel it would be best for the family if we moved west, and start a new life. I hear there is land to be had in the West by simply settling on it, and claiming a homestead.

"I feel we can get a good price for the farm now, but if we wait, I think there will be a hard times and we couldn't get much. I was offered three thousand dollars for the farm yesterday by a land speculator. I think we should take it. He said he would even give us time to sell our livestock, and all the implements and house furniture. People are in need of these things now, as they didn't manufacture anything but war material during the war, and there is a shortage of all these.

"What do you think, Mama?"

"We will follow you Papa, you are the wisest, and know more than we do. Things have changed so much, that there's little to stay for. You talked of California once, should we go there?"

"That is surely a possibility. Let's just see how the trip goes, and make up our minds when it's necessary."

It was settled and they sold everything they had, except for their clothes and their keepsakes, pulse the family Bible.

Ben's father had planned the whole trip. They would take a train to Chicago, then another south to St. Louis. From there they could go by boat to Kansas City. It had been advertised that a wagon train was forming there. It was a storybook trip that they all enjoyed.

The first day Ben asked his father, "Will I always be little. Here I am nearly fourteen years old and not five feet, yet. I weigh less than a hundred pounds."

Ben's father laughed and said, "It was the same for me, Ben. I was just your size until I was fifteen, then I grew like a weed. One summer I grew four inches, and put on twenty pounds. It was pure muscle, too, because my pa worked me hard. You'll grow, just be patient. One thing you have is your mom's thick auburn hair, and you have her nice skin, too. That will help you later in life. Your two sisters take after me in looks."

During the trip Ben's father talked to him a lot. He always emphasized keeping the family together as the top priority. He said, "Ben, one of the things you have to have to keep a family together is the love of Jesus Christ. If you are to lead a family, Christ must be at the center of it. A strong belief will keep a family together. The Bible teaches you how to do that. Remember how we read a chapter of Proverbs each day? There are thirty-one chapters, one for each day of the month. Proverbs gives a family something to live by. If you are the leader of a family, you must lead the family by example. They will most likely take after you, especially, if you show a good example.

"Money is another thing. If a family is hungry, it could split apart. Mother and I always set aside savings, even when times were bad. If you have something set aside for a rainy day, you can keep your family safe. Mother and I always paid the Lord first, but then paid ourselves, also. There are so many things I want you to know, Son. My father never got around to telling me these things, and I suffered learning them the hard way. Your mother knew a lot of the things my father should have told me, so she kept me out of trouble many times. Always listen to others' opinion with an open mind, before you make up your mind." Ben loved to hear his father's instructions and paid close attention to him.

The trip to Chicago was wonderful for Ben and his two younger sisters. They never tired of looking out the windows and seeing the countryside. In Chicago they marveled at the size and number of buildings. They spent a day sight seeing.

They then caught a train, and went south to St. Louis. At St. Louis they took a riverboat to Kansas City.

In Kansas City, Ben's father had made arrangements to join a wagon train going to California. They bought a Conestoga and four good mules. They loaded bedding, pots and pans and a large food supply. The wagon had two large water barrels strapped to its side.

Ben's father had bought two lever action rifles. One for him and one for Ben. He also bought a hundred rounds of ammunition. He carried a handgun with a scabbard that hung onto a belt. The belt held may rounds of ammunition.

One of the things Ben's father did, was to build a box under the seat, which he and Ben sat on while driving the mules. In the box was their valuables, Ben's rifle, the ammunition along with the family bible. It also contained an extra canteen, and a sack of jerky for emergency use.

His father had been told there would be over a hundred and twenty wagons, but just over fifty showed up. The wagon master told them the reason for the others not showing up, was because of a plague of cholera. It had infected most of the wagon train that was coming from the southeast. The wagon master explained that he couldn't wait on the other train, as it would take all their time to reach California before the snow fell in the Sierra mountains.

Because of having just over fifty wagons in the wagon train, Ben's father thought about not going, but the wagon master assured him that fifty wagons could hold off any band of Indians. They even practiced forming a circle when the wagon master shot three times quickly. He did this about every other day until they got it down.

Each night, after the wagons were in a circle, and the mules were watered, his father would take Ben and teach him to shoot his rifle. Ben was a quick study, and became pretty good. They would also hustle firewood on their trips to and from the practice. Once Ben shot an antelope, and was really proud.

Eight weeks into their trip they were attacked by Indians. The Indians had crept up on them with the majority of the tribe hidden behind a rise. The scout had been ambushed, and had no time to fire a warning shot. The wagon master was out front and they shot him, so he couldn't fire the warning shots to circle the wagons.

Upon hearing the shots, the wagons started to close up, and started the circle, but it was too late. Over seventy Indians hit the wagon train. There was a bloody fight.

Ben was trying to get into the box to get his rifle. He had just grasped the barrel when his mother was hit by a bullet. She inadvertently pushed Ben into the box with her body, the lid came down and her body kept Ben from getting out. When Ben's father could see that they would all be killed, he turned and shot his two girls just before an Indians killed him.

Ben could tell that the Indians had killed his family, so he remained silent in the box. The Indians set fire to all the wagons. Ben could smell the smoke. He knew to kick his way out would mean instant death. He then thought, *"I will be with my family shortly,"* then laid back and relaxed.

However, as the Indians were taking scalps, they saw a huge thunderhead coming with a tornado a quarter of a mile wide. They had seen this weather many times, and knew of its danger. They took the scalps, guns and ammunition, and ran for their horses. Several of them had already gathered all the mules and horses of the wagon train that were still alive, and fled south driving the horses and mules.

The tornado hit the ground, but bounced over the wagon train, and then hit the ground again. The Indians had left going south as fast as they could ride. They thought that the great sprit may be angry with them, so they left the area.

Ben was getting hot because by now, his wagon was engulfed in a raging fire. However, a torrential rain came, that completely extinguished the flames of his wagon and many others. He could hear the rain and wondered about the Indians. He waited until the rain had waned some. It was now deathly quiet except for the patter of rain. He then tried to get out of the box, but his mother's body blocked the door. Ben put his back to the back wall and drew his knees up, so his feet would have the maximum force. He was then able to move his mother enough to get out of the box.

When he came out, he saw his sisters, father and mother were dead and scalped. He was shocked, but he sat down to think as he remembered his father's words. He had said, *"Ben, when tremendous catastrophes happen to you, sit and think before you act. Take the time to relax and think out your next move. That way, you will nearly always make the right decisions."*

Ben knew he had to leave, and be on his way. He thought of the direction he should go. He thought the nearest civilization would be west, as they were headed. However, where were the Indians, and would they come back? He thought he would check their tracks, and see where they went. They had gone south, and he could tell by the length of the horses strides that they were running full out.

He then thought about the money his father carried. He looked through his father's wallet and it contained about a hundred dollars. He kept the wallet, and put it in his back pocket. He went back to the box he had been trapped in, and found the small tin box that held the family's valuables. The box contained over three thousand dollars mostly in paper money. As he looked at all that cash, he wondered about the other families valuables.

Most of the wagons had been burned badly, however, none were completely burned. He was able to find the hiding places of many of them, because the rain had doused the fire. He began to see he would need a bag as there was so much money. He found a cloth valise and began loading the money into it. He could then see that he could not take all the money especially the gold and silver coins, they would be much too heavy.

He found a large iron box in one of the wagons. It contained five thousand dollars. Some of it was in gold and silver coins. He dragged it over to a large rock that was on the edge of the rise the Indians had hidden behind. As he was filling the valise with money he found a backpack and started putting the large bills in the backpack. He put all the gold and silver coins in the iron box and then went back to get the rest of the money from the wagons.

He worked for four hours before he had all the money from the wagons, because he took his time. It took him some time to find the hiding place for the money of the many wagons, but he always found it. Generally it was in a tin box like his family used. Ben then went through the pockets of the men and found a lot more money. Most of it was paper, as few men weighted themselves with coins.

He now had all the money, and sat down to count it. He just made a quick count and could tell there was a couple of thousand gold and silver coins, but the majority was in paper money. He counted out fifty-thousand-four-hundred in bills. It was a heap of money.

He decided to take some hundreds and fifties, then a lot of twenties, tens and fives. He would only take about thirty of the ones as they would take up too much space in his backpack. He filled the backpack about a third full of the paper money, and put the rest in the large iron box.

He then thought of the rings, watches and bracelets. If left, the Indians would get them, so he went back and started taking those. This took another hour. He saw several diamond rings and put two of them in his backpack. The rest he dumped into the iron box. The box was large, but it now was nearly full of money rings and watches. The coins had made it too heavy to lift, but he had it beside the place he would bury it.

He took a shovel and began to dig. He buried it deep and partially under the largest rock on the ridge. He then pushed the large box into the hole and covered it up. He placed other rocks on top of the filled hole so that it looked like the ground around it.

Ben then stood back and surveyed the area, so if he ever came back, he would have little trouble recovering the box. He knew the area now and knew he could find the area again when needed.

He then went to his wagon and began to dig a grave for his family. He dug just one hole. He wrapped each in a blanket and began covering it. He thought that no one would ever find them. He said a prayer, then put on his hat and went into the wagon to prepare for his trip. He made a mental list of the things he would need.

He had good shoes. His father had bought them in St. Louis. They were brogans that came up past his ankles. He would need his hat, but he had seen the hat Mr. Oliver had worn. It was made of beaver skin and was very nice.

The paper money would be at the bottom of the sack with the family Bible on top of the bills. He thought of extra clothes, but he could buy them when he arrived at a community if he needed them. He put in the sack of jerky, a fire making kit, although he had a box of matches. He put in two cans of peaches, that he liked, a bag of beans, a small pot, a coffee pot, a cup and a tin eating pan. He then poured in all the extra ammunition and rolled up two blankets in his slicker, a ground clothe, with his rifle in the middle. He tied them to the top of his backpack. He lifted the pack to measure its weight. It weighed about fifteen pounds. He strapped it on and started walking west.

He then saw a hatchet and put it in his belt next to his sheath knife. He stopped and picked up Mr. Oliver's hat and wore it over his.

It was now dark, but the sky had cleared and a large moon was rising behind him. It produced enough light for him to travel with ease. He walked until about midnight and found a running stream. Along its bank he found an overhang, and decided this was a good place to camp. His fire could not be seen, and there was driftwood in the area. He found some kindling and some buffalo chips, and started a fire. He took some water from the stream and put it in his coffee pot along with some jerky he shaved to make a broth. He let that boil while he laid out his bedroll. After he had drank his soup and ate a piece of jerky, he laid on his blankets, and looked up at the stars. He tried not to think of his folks, but rather to concentrate on his task at hand, getting to civilization. He then thought of all the money he had. He decided to get an exact count of it tomorrow. Out on the plains, the money was not useful at all.

Chapter 2

CHIEF LEE

He was up at daybreak and decided that he should travel when it was cool. He traveled until noon, and came to some bushes that gave him shade. He used his hatchet to cut the ground out so that he would have a cool place to lie. He hadn't slept much the night before, so he was asleep in minutes. When he woke, he looked at the sun. It was now above the horizon only two hands high in the west. That meant that there was only about two hours left of sunlight. His father had taught him how to use his hand by pointing at the sun, then measuring the hand widths to the horizon to count the number of hours left in the day.

The weather had cooled some, so he packed up and began walking. At times the grass was nearly over his head. His fourteen year-old body was below the grass, and it was hard for him to find his way. He used the sun as his marker Ben was used to walking. He had walked beside the wagon picking up buffalo chips for the evening fire, since they had been on the plains.

Around noon, he found some tall grass and put his ground cover over it. It weighed it down some, so it couldn't be readily seen. He made him a small place with his hatchet and it was a cool place to sleep. He wasn't that hungry, but he ate a piece of jerky anyway. He then thought of the money. He emptied his backpack and counted the money. There was over twelve thousand dollars. He remembered he had left much more paper money in the box than was in his pack. He was rich! Every wagon had a lot of cash. He then thought of the iron box with all the other money, plus the gold and silver coins. That was a good reserve. He may someday really need money, and if he did, he knew where to find it. He studied the diamond rings. One was of good size, but the other was rather small.

He came to a stream the next day and just in time, as he was out of water. His canteen held about a half-gallon, but on a hot day, he could easily drink that. He washed himself all over. The cool water felt good. He dried himself and went to sleep. When he woke he wondered how many miles he covered each day. He then thought, *"I wish I had brought a map. Dad had one somewhere."*

He had seen his dad step to measure a distance. He had about a three foot stride, but Ben thought his stride was only two feet. He then thought, *"I could have brought a watch. When I get up, I will measure the hours until sundown and count my steps. I could then get an idea of how many miles I cover."*

He was now down to less than half-full of water, and knew he must get some water soon. That night he drank and ate one of the tins of peaches. He woke the next morning and was on his way before the sun broke the horizon. He had only walked about an hour, when he saw what looked like a man just sitting with his back to him. As he approached the man, he could see it was an Indian without a hat. He did wear a feather in his hair.

Ben approached cautiously. He saw no weapons on the man, and wondered if he were alive. He walked around the Indian and said, "Good morning. Do you speak English?"

The Indian said, "Yes, may I have some water?"

Ben handed him his canteen and the Indian drank only a small sip, then another then another. He then handed the canteen back to Ben.

Ben sat down opposite of the Indian and said, "I'm Ben Carson, who are you?"

"I am Lesta Katonka. It means little buffalo."

"Why are you sitting here, Mr. Lesta Katonka?"

"My tribe left me here. One of the young warriors' horse went lame. He threw me off my horse and took it. His horse was not that bad, but he lead him away. They took everything I had, and left me here to die. I have sang my death song, so I am ready."

"You are not that old. I think we should form our own tribe. You will be called Chief Lee. I will be called Ben Lee. When we get more warriors, they will be called Lee, also. You are now a chief. Where will we go now, Chief Lee?"

Chief Lee smiled at Ben and said, "That is a kind thought, Ben Lee. You are a great warrior."

"No, a little brave, but I feel we will be many and strong. We need to move. Here, Chief, take this hat and this hatchet." Ben handed the chief Mr. Oliver's hat and the hatchet. "They are yours. I will give you some jerky."

Ben reached into his pack and pulled out two pieces of jerky. The chief rose while he ate the meat, and they continued west.

Around noon they came to a small stream and they rested. Ben filled the canteen first, then drank deeply. He then took the coffee pot and shaved up a piece of jerky with the water. The chief watched him, as he built a fire and gathered buffalo chips to fuel it. He also found some driftwood along the small rill.

The chief said, "Where will we get the warriors, Ben Lee?"

"They will come, Chief. God will provide."

Ben then asked, "How do you talk such good English, Chief Lee?"

"I learned it in a school led by missionaries. I went through nine years."

"My, that's more schooling than I have.

"Are you a Christian, Ben Lee?"

"Yes, are you?"

"Many years ago, I was in the mission, and they taught me about Jesus. I believe in him. He is the Son of the Great Spirit. However, we were starving so I went with the others, and we began to raid. I knew it was wrong, but I went along with the others. They could see I would not kill, so they began to make fun of me. Later, they turned me out of their tribe. I went back to the mission, and it was good for awhile. I worked in the fields. I married and had two children.

"However, the priests were driven out by some of the white men, and we were put on our own. The Kiowa raided our village and took my wife and killed my children. They did the same to others, so we again became warriors. We gathered with others, and made a mighty force. We killed and burned all the white people we could. I tried to cover the fact that I would not kill, but some began to suspect.

"I was the best horse thief, and was respected for that. I could slip into a camp, and take a horse while they were guarded. Horses have a strong sense of smell. I always took my clothes and rubbed them on the horses. I learned to talk softly to them, and they were friendly to me.

"I never looked at taking horses as stealing, because they belonged to the Indians, before they did the white man.

"I would wait until the person guarding the horses was drowsy, and then I would slip in and speak into the ears of the horses. I would then loose one of them, and undo the rope holding the others. I would lead the one horse away softly. The others would then pull away, and begin to follow. By morning the horses were all over the range.

"When I was not as strong as I used to be, the young warrior took my horse and you found me the next day."

"That is all in the past, now, Chief. We will have a mighty tribe again. It will not start right away, but the tribe will grow."

They were running out of food, but the chief knew how to set snares. He was able to snare rabbits and small animals. He taught Ben how to live off the land, and enjoyed teaching Ben.

They didn't talk much when they traveled, but Ben asked, "Is there a town or village somewhere near?"

"Yes, we should be coming to one in a day or two." The next day they came to the village. It only contained about a hundred people. The village had been much larger at one time, but was now dwindling. There was a livery stable, saloon, hotel, café, general store and a few houses. As they approached they saw one of the houses near a stream was empty. Its windows were gone and the door ajar.

Ben said, "Let's use this as our home. He found a broom, and started cleaning the place. The chief joined in, and in about an hour they had it looking tolerable. They found some dishes in the cupboard and there was a table and four chairs. There was a fireplace that had an iron cooking device on it.

Ben said, "There is no firewood. We will have to go gather some." The village sat near a creek that ran year round. There were many cottonwoods growing, and Ben was off to gather wood. It was late afternoon when Ben went to the general store. He was the only customer.

The owner said, "You're new in town. Where's your family?"

"We're camped in that abandoned shack down by the creek."

"Yes, that was the Darby place, but they up and taken out for Denver, as there was nothing here to hold them. No one owns it, I think. There are no windows and it's in gross disrepair, so I suppose you can squat there. What's the name of your family?"

"We're the Lee's. I'm Ben and we call the old man, chief."

"That is not very respectful, young man."

"Oh, he's part Indian and he's called Chief Lee."

He looked at Ben with a jauntiest eye, but made no comment. He then said, "How may I help you, Ben?"

Ben bought two lamps and a bottle of kerosene. He then bought groceries and paid with a five dollar bill. The owner said, "My, we don't get many of these."

Ben said with a grin, "We don't either," and the owner laughed.

Ben's arms were full when he returned. Chief Lee had started a fire and had water boiling. Ben handed him some coffee and some side meat. They had potatoes, tomatoes, onions and some beef steak. He also had a dozen eggs and ten pounds of flour, some sugar and salt.

The chief was a good cook. He told Ben he had helped a cook at the mission. There he had learned the white man's way of cooking, and now preferred it to Indian cooking. It was the first decent meal they had in sometime, so they ate hardily. After they ate, Ben went back to the general store to buy some cloth to hang over the windows.

As he was going back to the store, he saw a girl about his age sitting on the edge of the boardwalk crying. Ben stopped and sat down beside her. She looked over at Ben and he put his arm around her. She began to cry again and clung to Ben. When she quieted some, Ben said, "It's okay. I've come to help you."

"The girl looked at him and said, "Are you an angel?"

"No, but I was sent by one."

"I just prayed for God to send an angel prayed for God to send an Angel to help me, and just at that moment you sat down beside me. I have never had God answer my prayers until tonight."

Ben said, "Do you have a family?"

"No, I was sold to Mr. Baker, who owns the eating house, by two raw-hiders who owned me. They were going onto the plains to shoot buffalo, and needed shed of me. I think they were tired of me. They saw the café, and saw that Mr. Baker had no help, so they offered me to him for twenty-five dollars. Mr. Baker made the deal. He had a bath tub and took me in there and scrubbed me down all over. He then bought me this dress, as the one I was wearing was filthy. He cut my hair some and tried to purty me up to attract customers. I earned my keep as I waited on table and washed all the dirty dishes before I went to bed. Mr. Baker used me like the raw-hiders did, but he was more gentle.

A day or two ago, I began getting these sores on me. They itched, but I didn't scratch them, as I was afraid that they would become infected. Mr. Baker saw the sores, and kicked me out. I was just sitting here praying, when you sat down beside me. Will you help me?"

"Of course, that's why I'm here. Let's go into the store and buy you some clothes and some medicine. I'll ask Mr. Carlyle if he has anything for your sores."

Ben said, "Mr. Carlyle, do you have anything to help this girl. She is developing sores all over her."

Mr. Carlyle, laughed and said, "She has the chicken pox. They're going around. I have some soap and medicine that will help her. In three or four days they will start to go away. Nearly everyone has had the chicken pox. He gave Ben some medicine, and told him to bathe her with a special soap he had. Ben then picked up some regular soap and three towels. He also bought her some underwear, some pants like men wore, a shirt and some sturdy shoes and good socks. He bought three more blankets and handed Mr. Carlyle another five dollar bill.

Mr. Carlyle said, "I hope you and your family will stay with us for many months. I haven't had anyone with your kind of money in weeks."

"I would ask you not to tell anyone we have cash. We would be robbed for sure."

Mr. Carlyle said, "I won't say a word to anyone. If I can help you in anyway just call on me."

On the way back to their shack Ben said, "My name is Ben Lee. I live with Chief Lee. He's an Indian, but he's a Christian and a nice person."

"I'm Cary Elders. My family was going west and ran out of money. I was the oldest, and Papa told me he had to sell me, or the rest would starve. I looked at Mama, and she was skin and bones, as were my two sisters. I told him I would be glad to help the family. He sold me to a drummer named Milton Evers. He was heading to Cheyenne. He used me like a saloon woman. I had never been with a man before, but he was gentle and treated me nicely. He didn't love me or I him, but I considered myself married. However, in Cheyenne he got into a poker game, and lost all his money. He came back to our wagon that night and told me he was sorry, but he had to sell me to two raw-hiders. I was sad, but understood. The two raw-hiders were rough with me, and both did me several times a day. It was very bad, but I endured. They didn't feed me much. By the time we got here, they were both tired of me, and didn't want me anymore. That's when they sold me to Mr. Baker. You know the rest."

"Well Cary, your new name is Cary Lee. Chief Lee was thrown out of his tribe and my folks were killed by Indians. We decided to form a new tribe, and you are our newest member."

"I'll work hard, Ben. I can do a lot of things mama taught me. I will be your woman and treat you good. Will the chief want me, too?"

"No, Cary. The chief and I are Christians, and we hold to the laws of God. You will be your own woman. When we get to the house, I will take you to the creek, and you can bathe with the soap that Mr. Carlyle sold us. I will then put the medicine on you.

They arrived at the house and Ben said, "Chief, this is our latest member of our tribe. Her name is Cary Lee. We must now leave to bathe."

The chief said, "I will make you a supper, Cary Lee. Welcome to our tribe."

When they arrived at the creek, Cary began to disrobe. She looked at Ben and said, "Don't be embarrassed, you need to help me bathe. If I am a member of the tribe, we don't have to be shy about being nude."

Ben thought, "*What the heck, I've bathed with my sisters, so she is a sister, too.*" Ben then took off his clothes, and they bathed. Ben washed her back and hair. He made sure he bathed every inch of her body with the special soap. She then washed his back.

As Ben was applying the medicine to her soars with a piece of cotton he had bought to apply the medicine, he said, "I think we will be a good family. We will pray together, and will honor Jesus with everything we do. Like now, we are both nude, but we know that we do so with no sin."

Cary smiled and said, "I think I am in heaven, and you and the chief are angels. My life has started anew."

After they were dressed they returned to house. The chief had made her a good supper. Before they ate, Ben said, "Shall we pray?" They all bowed their heads and Ben said, "Lord, we are starting a family. Each one of us has had terrible things happen to us, but we know that it is all in your plans. We are here together, so please let us form a loving family that will honor you. Thank you for our latest member, Cary. Our faith in you will grow, and we will become stronger. Bless the food especially for Cary. Please heal her, in the name of Jesus, I offer this prayer to you, Father."

Cary was crying again, so the chief put his hand on her shoulder and said, "Welcome to the tribe, Cary Lee."

Chapter 3 ════════════════════════════

THE STAGE COACH

They decided to stay another day or so to decide where they should go. They knew that this place was not going to be their home. Ben talked of getting some acres themselves so they could raise their own animals and crops. He bought a map and they all studied it.

Ben asked about Cheyenne, but Cary said, "I was only there a short time. We were just passing through. It's a town like this, but a little bigger and rougher. I surely don't want to live there, if we can help it."

Ben said, "We need to stay here until your sores clear up. I will bathe you everyday, and keep you as clean as we can. I will buy you another outfit. You will need a dress and some ladies shoes. You should also have a bonnet."

Cary said, "You are too good to me, Ben."

"It's not just me, it is what a family should do." Ben gave each of them three dollars. He said, "Everyone should have some walking around money. It just makes a body feel better to know he's not broke. Chief, I want to buy you white men's clothes so they will not pick on you. With these clothes and your hat, everyone will just think we are a family."

They bought fishing lines and hooks, and enjoyed fishing. The Chief always went to bed when it was dark, but Cary and Ben liked to walk in the cool night air and talk. She said, "I only went to school through the third grade. I can read and write and cipher enough, so as to make change. I know my English is bad, You and the chief seem to talk like educated men, Ben. Try to correct my bad English. I don't want to embarrass you."

Ben laughed and said, "You could never do that, you are my sister."

She then stopped and hugged him. She said, If I am to be your sister, I can hug you anytime I want to, and I'll want to a lot."

Ben said, "That is the first hug I've had since mama was killed."

Cary hugged him again and said, "I will be both mama and sister to you, and someday, I may give you children."

Ben stopped and said, "We're too young to think of that, Cary. I have urges that way, but I must control them."

Cary said, "We can talk about anything together. This is how I think everyone should be, but I know in polite company, we could never mention things like that. I feel the same way at times, and like you, I will try to control my urges. I would like to sleep with you every night, but I know where that would lead."

Ben smiled at her candidness. She seemed to look at sex just as a normal body function, and talked about it as such.

As they were coming back, Mr. Baker was throwing a customer out. He only had one arm. Baker said, "And stay out." Baker was a brute of a man. He was over six feet and weighed over two-fifty. He enjoyed making lesser men knuckle under.

The man was wearing a Confederate soldier's uniform, that was worn. He sat on the edge of the boardwalk with his head in his hands. Ben winked at Cary, and she got the message. They both sat on each side of him and Cary said, "An angel sent us to help you, Mister."

Ben said, "That's right. You need help, and we are the ones who will do it. Please come with us."

The man was completely amazed and said, "Where did you come from?"

"We came from heaven, just come with us. The man rose and followed them. When they arrived at the shack Ben called, "Chief Lee, we have another member of our tribe. He's hungry and tired."

The chief lit a lamp, and started fixing a supper for the man. They still had coffee on, and Cary fixed him a cup. Ben then said, "The man fixing your supper is Chief Lee. That is Cary Lee and I'm Ben Lee. What is your name."

The man then smiled and removed his hat. He was a handsome man about thirty or younger. He was about six feet in height, and weighed about a hundred and eighty pounds. He said, with a southern drawl, "I'm Captain, well ex-captain, Robert Ward. I had saved a goodly amount of money, and bought a stage ticket to Denver. I was trying to get to California to start a new life. I lost my wife and my arm during the war. One to another man and the other to cannon fire. When my wife saw I only had one arm, she left me. I then learned she was seeing another man while I was away. So, I thought I would come west. However, when I arrived here, they told me that the stage line could not go to Denver, as they couldn't get drivers to go because of the Indian trouble. I tried to get a refund on my money, but they said that they would take me back, but could not refund my money.

"I got a room at the hotel and went to their café for dinner that night. I went to bed about ten, and didn't wake until this afternoon. I found that I had been robbed and that I was broke. I went to find the sheriff, but was told that he lived in Cheyenne and was a U. S. Marshal. They have no local authority. I went to have dinner, and the owner of the café was also the owner of the hotel. He threw me out as he already knew I had been robbed."

Cary said, "He used knockout drops on you, then robbed you. He's done it before. The cook told me to watch what I drank as he puts the drops in coffee when some stranger is staying at his hotel, and looks like he has money."

"Well, he took my pistol too, and with only one arm what am I to do about it?"

Before he ate, Ben offered a prayer welcoming him to their family. Ben said, "You are now in the Lee tribe. Your name is now Robert Lee."

Robert laughed and said, "That fits."

Cary said, "What I should do, is sneak into his café late tonight after he is in bed and swipe the knockout drops. I know where he keeps them. I can then change the bottle with a bottle that looks just like it and put water in it. The next time he tries to rob someone he may get his head shot off," and they all laughed.

The next day they bought more blankets and Cary asked for a bottle. Mr. Carlyle showed her a number of bottles. She knew just the one she wanted.

Ben addressed Mr. Carlyle and asked, "I noticed a stage just sitting out back of the stage line. Is it being used?"

"No, Ben, the owner of the stage line just closed up and went to Cheyenne."

"Can we just take it?"

"As far as I'm concerned you can. The law says, that anything abandoned can be used by anyone, like you all using that shack."

After they left, Ben said, "We could buy some horses at the livery, and use that stage to travel in. We could store all our goods. It'll be a great way to travel."

"What about the Indians?" Robert asked.

"We'll just have to take that risk, if we are to travel west or north. We need to decide that tonight."

Robert said, "My arm is only gone to the elbow. I can still use a rifle. I used to be pretty good with a rifle."

Ben said, "My dad showed me how to shoot."

Cary said, "My father showed me also, so we could be a force with three rifles."

Ben said, "Chief, if it were to defend your family could you shoot?"

"Yes, I think the Lord allows that." I can shoot. We will need three more rifles."

They discussed it at length. They had bought some excellent maps that showed the terrain, as well as the trails. They finally decided to go to Denver.

After everyone was asleep that night, Cary slipped out of the shack and used a window that was never locked in the kitchen of the café. She swapped the bottle with water in it, for the one with the knockout drops and never said a word about it to anyone.

The next day they bought three rifles and a handgun with a scabbard for Robert. He began teaching all of them to shoot, better. Ben helped. They bought more ammunition than Ben thought they needed, but he didn't say anything.

Robert asked Ben, "Where are you getting all the money for the things we use?"

Ben said, "My folks saved up a few hundred dollars. When they were killed I just took it, and came on west. Can you buy us some good animals to pull the stage, Robert?"

"Yes, I know horses. I was talking to the chief about that. He knows horses, also. So we will go to the stable tomorrow, and see what we can do. You had better come with us, as you have all the money."

Ben said, "Why don't you get some new clothes. That uniform is worn."

"I hate to take money from you, Ben."

"It's not just my money, it's the tribes' money now."

Robert smiled and took the money. He came back with new clothes on and new boots. However, he kept his Confederate hat.

At the livery stable, they found that the horses that had pulled the stage were still there and were fine horses. They made a deal with the man as he really didn't own them, so he gave them the horses for what was owed him.

"They re-branded the horses as the Bar Lee. The hostler said, "When you get to Denver register your brand with the government.""

Mr. Carlyle sold them everything they would need for the trip, and one cool morning they were off. Ben drove the stage as he had handled his wagon's team many times. The chief sat with him and they were off.

***

The day they left, unbeknown to the Lee family, a rider came into the town. He was a handsome young man dressed very well, but was not very big. His horse was the best and everyone who saw him knew he was well to do.

When the stranger turned in that night he took precautions and was a light sleeper. He had eaten at Bakers café and drank his coffee. He had a room upstairs in the hotel, and turned in about ten. As he was wary about strange places, he made his bed beside his bed between the wall and the bed. He put blankets so it looked like he was in bed.

Well after midnight, he heard his door open. He had his gun beside him. As the person came into the room, the prowler started going through the man's clothes. He found the man's wallet, but then heard the hammer of a six-gun being cocked and froze.

The man holding the gun said, "If you want to live until tomorrow, light that lamp on the table. Baker lit it, as he could see he was caught dead to rights. The man took Baker's gun and told him to stand in the corner, while he got dressed.

Baker said, "I'll give you a thousand dollars if you will just let me go. I have it in my safe downstairs."

After the man was dressed, he followed Baker downstairs and watched as Baker opened his safe. The man told Baker to stand back and the man emptied his safe which contained a little over eight thousand dollars. He then said, "I've got to punish you more than just taking your money. I'm going to tell everyone in the town what you tried to do. If you tell them I robbed you, I will come back and shoot you in both knees, so you will be a cripple for life. I don't really need your money. I think I might give it to someone who wants to build a hotel. The stipulation will be to charge his customer twenty-five cents less than you do for a room."

He went back to his room and went to sleep.

***

As they traveled, the chief was constantly looking for dust in the air. When he thought he saw some, they would slow and try to find a defendable place.

The first stop was at a way station for the stage. It was a small farm actually. When they pulled up. A man came out and said, "I thought the stage had quit. I got a letter saying my contract was cancelled. I have a good change of horses for you. Let me yell at ma to start supper."

No one said anything, then Ben said, "Shouldn't we tell him?"

Robert said, "Let's wait awhile, and let him enjoy the false hope. Everyone should have hope. I had none, until two angels sat beside me one night. You brought new hope within me. I've got new clothes now and new hope. I had no family, now I have the best in the world."

Ben grinned at him and said, "We were all in the same boat, Robert. You have a much different face than you did the night we found you. I believe God delivered you to us. Our family is much better now."

The man came out and introduced himself. He said, "I'm Homer Dobbs and my Misses is Alta. We have three kids and the oldest is Sarah. She was hoping to go to Denver to see her aunt, but the stage stopped coming. Isolated out here, she might never catch a husband. Come on in and meet my family.

They came into a clean house. Alta was standing by the kitchen door and three children were in line. Sarah was the first. She wasn't a child, she was at least twenty, and the two boys were in their late teens. Sarah immediately looked at Robert, as he was handsome. Her heart leaped, then she saw he had but one arm. This made her think, *"He could never make a livin' with one arm, but he is handsome."*

Alta broke the silence by saying, "You can wash up over younder." She pointed to three ewers with bowls on a counter across the dining room. They all washed up, then were seated at a table with a tablecloth. The plates were nice china and the glasses were standing by them with cool water in them.

The meal was chicken and dumplings with green beans and summer squash. They were all very hungry. Ben stood and said, "Would you allow me to ask thanks to our Lord?"

Homer said, "By all means."

Ben prayed for their safe trip and asked for the Lord to keep his hand on the Dobbs' family and keep them safe. He then thanked him for the Dobb's family, and ended by asking God to bless the food and the hands that prepared it.

Homer said, "You're a right smart talkin' young man, you should be a sky pilot. How old are you, eleven or twelve?"

Ben said, "I'm small for my age. I'm actually almost fourteen. However, the Lord has been so good to each one of us, that I want to thank him ever so often. You see we are a family. The Lee family, as a matter of fact. That is Chief Lee, a great leader of men; Captain Robert Lee, Cary Lee and myself, Ben Lee."

"You mean that Indian is a member of your family?"

"As much as anyone of us. As a matter of fact, it was he who was wise enough for us to travel safely. He has a sixth sense about enemies."

"Well, I'll be. You have the strangest family I ever heared of."

"Where is the stage driver?"

Robert said, "That is something we need to explain. You see, we own this stagecoach. It's not the Emerson Stage Line. We own it, and are traveling to Denver, and maybe to California. We would, however, be honored to take your beautiful daughter to her aunt. There is danger though, as many Sioux are making raids. As a matter of fact, you are in danger just living here."

"I know that, Sonny Boy, however, I have dealt fairly with them Injuns and furnished them a beef now and again, when they ask. They have placed a sign over our gate that shows we are their friends."

Chief Lee said, "That was our way, but the new warriors now bring death to every one with white skin. You should come with us, and return when the army comes back. They have been too busy with the war, and have not paid much attention to the Sioux for sometime. The tribes are now joining together to run the white man back to the east. No one will be safe."

Homer was shocked. He said, "You mean they won't honor their sign. I thought an Indian never broke his word."

"That is true, an Indian does not break his word. But these are younger warriors, who did not give their word. They think their fathers are soft, and that is why the white man remains in their land. You know it is their land. The white man just came and took the land without asking them. You would do the same if someone came and took your farm."

Homer stroked his chin and said, "No one's movin' me off this farm, however," and he looked at Alta and said, "You and the boys should go with Sarah to your sisters. I'll make out here. I have hiding places where I can hole up for weeks if need be. The dogs will let me know when the Indians are near. I will just hole up until they leave."

Chief Lee said, "They will burn you out and take or kill all your animals including the dogs. Then how will you live."

"I'll make out, Chief."

Both boys said, "We'll stay with you, Pa."

Homer said, "No, both you and I will be safer if you go. You boys can ride our two best horses and bring along the extra team for the stage. If the Sioux cuts your trail, they'll see the many horses and maybe back off. I'll scatter the cows and turn the hogs loose. The chickens can make out as they always do."

Homer then said, "How is it that you speak English so well, Chief?"

I was schooled in a mission for nine years. I have even written some poems. I'm not a white man, but I was raised as a white man. I know the Indians though, because I rode with them. I was thrown out of one tribe because I would not kill. I told them my God did not allow me to do that. Several years later, I rode again with others, but I was past my prime, and the others looked down on me."

"Then why are you called, Chief?"

"Ben Lee gave me that title. We both took new names at that time, and decided to form a new tribe. We call it the *Ghost Tribe*, because we are so few that we are invisible."

"Well, you are not so few now. How big do you want your tribe, Chief?"

"Hundreds. Ben and I want everyone to know the truths of Jesus Christ, and this is our way of doing that."

They stayed an extra day for the women to pack. Alta took the family Bible and all their valuables. Both boys were armed with rifles and a supply of ammunition. The older boy, Hank, wore a pistol and a scabbard low on his leg, and the gun was tied down at the bottom. The other boy, Barney, was very quiet and kept to himself.

They left at daybreak the second day. The boys rode good horses and were always out on their flanks looking for sign. This also kept down the dust some. The Chief was always looking over the horizon and would stop the stage at any sign of dust.

The stage coach now had five people in it. Sarah was inquisitive and wanted to know the history of everyone. This was a cover to get Robert's history. He told it in an abbreviated version leaving out the part about his wife leaving him.

Cary didn't tell them anything, however, they were inundated with the history of the Dobbs family and Alta's family, the Sanders, as Alta loved to talk.

Before they left, Ben asked Homer about the stage route. Homer had a map that showed the distances between each. The next station was twenty-seven miles away. It would take a good days ride to get there. Homer knew the water holes along the trail, and the distances to them, also. He marked them down on the map, and gave it to Ben. They all knew there was extreme danger along the trail.

The afternoon before they left, Robert explained what they must do when attacked. They were to leave the stage when he told them, and lie prone on the ground near it. He explained, "A soldier is less likely to be shot when he is lying in a prone position. You are also in a better position to steady and fire your weapon. Everyone is to carry extra shells with them. At least twenty. We will practice this maneuver this afternoon," which they did more than once. Robert knew his business about waging war. He was very happy to learn that both Alta and Sarah had experience firing a rifle.

Robert explained the reason for them lying next to the coach. He said, "An Indian cannot ride his horse over the coach, so it will give you protection. Ben you are to hitch the mules and horses to the coach. Make sure they are tied firmly, unless you can see a better place for them. Most of the time we will have some notification before an attack. We can then get to a better position, if there is one. If you are being overwhelmed. Yell, "Old Amy!' As loud as you can. When you hear someone yell 'Old Army,' you yell it, too. Then come to their aid, as soon as you can. We used this in battle, and it worked very well. Some of the men also used it in saloons, when they were outnumbered."

Chief Lee said, "Most times, warriors move in small groups, eight to twelve in a group. To feed a large number, warriors will require several animals and the hunting is not that good, so they spread out in small numbers."

Robert said, "Our number is eight, but we have repeating rifles. Most of the Indians aren't that well armed. If we follow the routine we practiced, we should do alright. The Indians will yell and scream as they attack. This is to make you afraid. Just think of them as wolves growling and barking. Be calm and methodical with your shooting. Never fire in haste, it does no good and wastes ammunition. Pick a target and squeeze the trigger. Remember, you have a partner on both sides of you. Think of them. It is your duty to keep your family from harm, and this is your family. Try only to think of protecting them."

Cary always spread her blanket near Ben. She said, "I'm scared, Ben. Please stay near me in a fight. Just knowing you are there helps me to no end."

Ben said, "Cary, you can always depend on me. I told Chief Lee the same thing, as I wanted him near me in a fight. He is steady and is not afraid. I wish I weren't, but I'm scared, too. With you on one side and the Chief on the other, what do I have to be scared about?"

Cary smiled then leaned over and kissed Ben on the cheek. No one slept very good the last night at Homer's farm. Each were in their own thoughts.

While they were practicing getting from the coach and getting into position, Homer watched Alta and thought, *"That there's a real woman. I have been so fortunate. I just hope we can all get through this."*

They left the next day and Ben knew every stop they would make. He always watered the horses himself. However, Cary would bring the extra horses and helped him. The trail was very plain, as the stage coaches of the past had made it a two rut trail. Ben watched carefully to make the ride as smooth as he could.

Chapter 4 ══════════════════════════════

DENVER AND BUSINESSES

They reached a stage station about thirty miles from Homer's farm. It was deserted. They stayed there that night by a small creek that had good grass on its banks. They staked the horses and decided to stay outside, as the station was filthy and infested with rats. Ben caught a couple of wild hens for their supper. Cary and Sarah found nests, and gathered several eggs for breakfast. They left early the next morning with a change of horses.

The next evening they came upon a small town on the Republican River. They decided to stay a day or two to rest up. Ben and Robert found a house for rent and talked the man into renting it to them for a dollar a day. It was empty and the man wanted five dollars for a week. Robert said, "We will go to the hotel, it will be cheaper, and be closer to town. As they turned to leave the man said, "Okay, I'll go for a dollar a day?"

Robert turned around and grasped his hand and said, "It's a deal." Ben paid him two dollars. They set up house there. It was near the river, and all of them took baths. They had soap and towels. They waited until dark and the women went first, then the men.

When they were all at the house, Alta said, "We need to do some hair cutting on you men." She had a sharp pair of scissors and started with her two boys. She then did Robert's hair and took particular time with him, as she was hoping Sarah would see something in him. Ben was next and she cut his hair short and neat. She then turned to the chief.

Ben said, "If you will cut your hair and wear your new clothes, you will look more like the rest of us, Chief." Everyone finally convinced him, and he had his hair cut short. He put on Mr. Oliver's hat, and he looked like a member of the family.

The next evening Cara and Ben went for a walk. It wasn't that late, but two cowboys were drunk and when they saw Cara, she was wearing a dress that made her look like a woman. The cowboys pushed Ben aside and grabbed Cara. Ben yelled, "Old Army!" as loud as he could. In less than two minute there were four people standing near the cowboys with rifles. Ben then said, "If you want to stay alive, you will unhand that girl and apologize to her."

One cowboy said, "Says who?"

Robert said, "The four rifles that are pointed at you."

The cowboys then saw they were surrounded. They dropped Cary and one said, "Just wait until we get our friends."

Hank came forward and said, "There is no need for that, unless you are not man enough to solve your own trouble."

The cowboy could see the tied down gun and the look on Hanks face. He knew he was in big trouble. His friend could see it too, and said, "We were drunk, no need to have a killing over it. We apologize and it will never happen again."

Hank said in an icy voice, "If I see you close to Miss Lee again, I will shoot either of you on sight."

The cowboys left. They worked for a small outfit that only had five cowboys. They knew this bunch was pure poison. One said to the other, "Don't mention this to anyone. If the others found out, they may turn on us, too. We did a stupid thing back there. I hope we both learned from it." They got their horses and returned to their ranch, which was at the edge of town.

After two days the women had washed all the dirty clothes, and the men had mended the tack and given the horses a good rest. The third day they were on their way at daybreak. They crossed the Republican river at an easy ford, and were now heading west for the Arkansas river. There was a stage station at the Arkansas river, according to the map.

About four that evening, the Chief saw dust and it was heading for them. Ben shouted at Robert as he brought the coach to a stop. They saw a group of rocks not far from them. After everyone was out of the coach, Ben pulled the coach on the other side of the rocks. Hank and Barney had heard the cry and saw the dust. They were back, and the horses were kept between the stage coach and the rocks.

When the riders were within three hundred yards they could see it was a cavalry patrol. They road up and the lieutenant said, "I see you are prepared for a fight. That is good to see. I thought the stage line was closed."

"It is" Robert said, "We own this coach. We are the Lee family."

We are pleased to meet you, Mr. Lee. You have a fine family. There are Indian bands roaming this area attacking small groups. I see they will have their hands full with you. I don't have to tell you people to be on the lookout, but be careful."

He tipped his hat and the patrol rode off. Everyone was relieved. They had an early lunch, and were on their way. Ben looked at the chief and said, "I would like to see more of those patrols."

The stage station at the Arkansas river had never closed. They received customers from the river travel. Canoes and an occasional long boat came to rest. The owner explained that most people came along the river, as some farms were being located there along with some villages.

They had a hot meal and spent the night in a bed. Cary made sure she was close to Ben and this warmed him as he was now very close to her.

The owner, a Mr. Gibson, told them they were now just seventy miles from Denver, and that they would have no trouble with the Indians in that area. It was dotted with farms and the trail was nearly a road. They made good time, and two days later they were at the outskirts of Denver. It appeared to be a large city of maybe a couple of thousand people. It seemed to be growing, mostly because of the Indian trouble. People felt safer with population around them.

They first searched for Alta's sister, but found she had died of a sickness that also took her husband. Their two boys had both left for the war and had not returned.

Robert said, "No worry, you're part of the tribe now." Sarah was glad she would be with Robert, as he had become dear to her. He didn't know this, but she thought she would let things happen as they would. She would see that she was near him most of the time.

They asked around where the Emerson Stage Line was located and went there. They found a rundown hotel that was boarded up. There were corrals behind the hotel and a barn. They found hay and corn in a storage room of the barn. The tack room contained four old saddles. Robert said, "Should we throw these out?"

Ben said, "No, give me a time with them, I may be able to restore them with some linseed oil. I saw pa do it once."

Ben and the boys cleaned the barn and provided feed for the horses. They stored the coach in the barn. The barn and hotel were supplied with water from a wooden elevated tank, which was fed from a windmill. The windmill was on their property, but also feed two other businesses. One was a livery stable that was also abandoned. The other was a store of some sort, but all the merchandise was gone.

While the men were cleaning the barn and taking care of the animals, the women were busy cleaning the small hotel. The hotel had three stories with a bathroom on each floor. It had twelve bedrooms, a lobby, a kitchen and an office. Three of the rooms were downstairs and nine were upstairs. They just cleaned enough to make it habitable.

When the men arrived, Robert said, "We should go to the courthouse tomorrow and register our brand and ask who owns the stage station."

Alta said, "Yes, and I would like to find out what became of my sister's property."

The next day they registered their brand, the *Bar Lee*. They then asked about the Emerson Stage Line hotel. The clerk directed them to the tax collector.

The tax collector told them that the taxes hadn't been paid for the last year and this year's tax was due. He said, "If you will pay the tax bill, you can lay claim to it. If no one contest you paying the taxes for a year, then you are the legal owner."

Ben asked, "How much is last years and this years taxes?"

The clerk took out a ledger and looked it up. It came to a hundred and twenty dollars. Ben took out his wallet and paid the man, who was astonished. The clerk asked, "What name is to be on your business?"

Ben said, "The Lee Hotel."

As the clerk was entering the new name, Robert said, "We noticed that the livery stable just east of the hotel is vacant and the store just to the west of the hotel is vacant. We are interested in them also."

The clerk said, "The livery stable has been vacant for five years. I'll give you a break there. If you will pay this year and last years taxes, it's yours."

Ben again said, "How much?"

"I'll settle for eighty dollars for that. Since the Indians have kicked up their heels, the livery business has been practically non-existent."

Robert said, "Could you give us a minute?"

They then huddled. Robert said, "With the war coming to a close, their will be troops coming west. They will drive the Indians out and travel will flow again. I think this is a bargain. The building and property are worth two to three thousand dollars. What do you think, Ben, it's your money?"

"No Robert it isn't just my money. We are a family, and should be prudent with our investments. What do you think, Alta?

Alta said, "I think Robert's right. Even if we don't run the livery stable we could maybe sell it, and make a huge profit."

They turned around and Ben said, "We'll take it." The clerk put the name as Lee's Livery Stable.

Ben said, "Now we would like to ask about the store just to the west of the hotel."

The clerk said, "Now that store has been empty three years, and there's not much property with it. If you'll pay fifty dollars for the taxes, I can put it into the Lee name. What name would you like it under?"

"Robert said, "Lee's General Store." Ben paid the clerk.

Alta said, "My sister died last year. She had a house on Chestnut street. What happened to the property?"

The clerk said, "I remember Mr. and Mrs. Sanders. They died of cholera. They had two sons, neither of which came back from the war. We were holding the property in case the boys showed up, but neither came back. I feel if they were coming back, they would have been here by now. The Sander's estate paid for the taxes and debts. There was enough to pay for their funerals, also. The rest went to pay most of the taxes of this year. It was a little lacking, but the council waved that. The family Bible is around here some place. Let me dig it out." He was gone a minute or so and returned. "He said, "Are you Alta Dobbs?"

Alta pulled out her identification, and showed it to the clerk. He then looked at her and said, "What's your name now, Madam?"

"What else, 'The Lee family,'" and they all smiled.

"The clerk said, "I think the Lees are buying up Denver little by little. It wouldn't surprise me that sometime in the future Denver will be known as Leesville," and they all laughed.

Back at the hotel, Sarah had a fresh pot of coffee, and they all sat down to discuss the mornings activities."

Ben said, "Robert, you have put us on the right track. I believe that in the near future, the Indian trouble may subside, and we can reestablish the livery stable and the stage line. We can make contracts with the stage stations and deliver horses to them as we go.

Robert said, "We may get a contract with the U. S. mail service, and maybe some banks. They're always transferring money because of the mines. We may work this into a lucrative business. As to that store next door. I think we should look around Denver and see what business may be needed. If we are the only ones supplying something, then we could make a go at it. We have enough people in our tribe to man nearly all the businesses, so hiring people will not be necessary for awhile.

Alta said, "The hotel will be our living quarters. We won't be able to fill all the rooms now, but with Ben and the Chief out there looking for the homeless, I'm sure they will fill up soon."

Chapter 5

HOMER'S DEFENSE

After the coach pulled out that morning, Homer knew he had a lot of preparations to make if he was going to stay alive. He had heard stories about the Sioux uprisings. The old Indians didn't want war, but the young bucks had their dander up, as the white man killed Indians indiscriminately when they wanted their land.

An old timer had sold him his farm and stage station, as it had become too much for him. His wife had died and his two boys had left for the war. He told Homer he had picked the place as it sat in a short cul-de-sac some two hundred yards deep with a mouth of only a hundred feet. The place was sheltered by limestone cliffs that rose over a hundred feet in height, providing shelter from the wind, cold in the winter and shade in the summer.

The old timer had built just a small stone house to live in until he got the contract for the stage station. The station sat at the front of the cul-de-sac adjacent to the trail going east and west on the flat prairie. Back of the station were corrals, a barn, a chicken coop and a yard which provided a space for a large garden. The cliffs of limestone were sheer. The stage line had built a frame building to accommodate the stage passengers. It had a kitchen, dinning room and six bedrooms. When his wife and boys were gone, the old man had used one of the bedrooms for himself.

When Homer came, he could see his family needed a large house. The small stone house, that sat behind the stage station, was inadequate for Homer's family. Homer had been a mason for a time and knew how to build with stone. There was an area at the back of the cul-de-sac that had a layer of limestone about eight inches thick that was exposed. Homer eyed this and knew he could build a large stone house for his family. He laid the foundation aligning it with the stage station, but leaving a space of twenty feet between the two buildings for access to the cul-de-sac and its features.

Homer's wife, Alta, wanted the house to have much light and be airy. Homer allowed for many windows and three doors. It never crossed his mind that they may have to defend his house against Indians. The army had a fort within ten miles, and the Sioux had moved north.

The first year he began building the house with the help of his two boys. They laid the foundation and then the walls. He made the ceilings twelve feet high, as he knew that would handle the heat better than the common eight foot ceilings. It took him nearly two years to complete the house. It was like a cave and stayed cool in the summer and warm in the winter like a cave.

The first year, the few Indians who had remained on the plains, showed up at the station hungry. Homer gave them a yearling, that he had planned to butcher himself, but he had two other yearlings and some hogs. The Indians were grateful. He planned to give them at least two yearlings each year in the dead of winter, when game was scarce. The Indians in turn had put a sign on the upper wall of the stage station, that other Indians would recognize as a sign of peace. They did live in peace until midway through the Civil War. Then the army pulled out of the fort, as the soldiers were needed in the war effort.

Across from the stage station was the prairie. The old timer used the area for farm land. The soil was good and rains had been good. The old timer had planted some of the land in alfalfa and some in corn. It was enough to winter the horses and livestock he kept. He ran a few head of cattle and raised some horses also.

Homer increased the farmland and now could store enough corn and hay to last out a long winter.

Before the old timer left, he showed Homer a hole about three feet in diameter in the cliff. It was some five feet off the ground. He said, "Keep your children away from this hole. It drops off into a cave. I have explored it some, but it has passageways, so a body could get lost very easily."

No one paid the hole any attention as it was five feet off the ground. Homer had leaned timber against it, so that it was covered. Now, Homer decided to explore the cave. He brought a ladder to the hole, a lantern and a length of rope. He tied the rope to the ladder and lowered himself into the cave. Just three feet into the hole it dropped down about five feet to a flat floor in a large room, about thirty feet by thirty feet, with a ceiling of over thirty feet in height. He lit the lantern and looked around. He could see passageways leading out of the room. He walked very cautiously and went into the largest passageway that began dropping down a gentle slope. He walked on and came to another room that was enormous. It had a large pool of water in it that was deep. Stalactites' and Stalagmites were everywhere. The thought passed his mind that he could house all his animals here, if a time came where he needed them safe.

He had seen all he wanted for the time being. He went back to his house and made some coffee, and sat and thought about the cave. He had some dynamite and if he made the hole to the cave large enough to get his livestock in, they would have a haven in times of trouble.

He took his star drill and a single jack to create holes for the dynamite. He knew just where to place them to create a hole three feet wide and five feet high, the height needed to reach the hole. It took him all day to get this done. He then set off the dynamite. It created just what he wanted, an entrance that was eight feet high and three feet wide. Of course he had to use his the single jack to smooth up the sides and bottom.

Using the timber he had used to cover the hole, he built a shed that would cover the entrance to the cave he had created. The door to the shed was about the same size as the entrance to the cave. He covered the cave entrance with a tarp and left the door of the shed open so that if someone were looking at it, they would just see an empty shed.

Homer stood back and looked at the shed with pride. He then brought wood into cave to fence off the other passageways. He hauled troughs for feeding, several bales of hay and five sacks of corn weighing over seventy pounds each.

He dragged in a barrel of kerosene and all the lamps he could spare. He even took the livestock in and out of the opening so they would be used to it, when he needed to house them there.

Homer then thought of his own needs. He used the furniture from the old timer's house to furnish the outer room as living quarters. He was now set, if an Indian war party came.

With time on his hands he decided to explore more of the cave. The old timer had told him of the numerous passageways, so he marked the way to the entrance by breaking off stalactites and pointing them toward the outer room. He found one tunnel that seemed to go upward. It was small, but he could stand as he walked. He must have traveled a quarter of mile on a upward trend when he saw some daylight. He was excited. It was a hole about two feet in diameter, and he crawled through it. He was on a ledge of the his cul-de-sac. He had seen the ledge, but thought nothing of it at the time, as it was seventy feet about the floor of the cul-de-sac. The ledge was slanted upward, so that no one could see the hole from below.

His thoughts went to using this place to discourage Indians from burning the station or coming into his house. Homer had extra rifles and a lot of ammunition. He decided to bring food and water to the ledge so he could man it for a day or two.

Homer now thought he was fairly prepared.

***

The Lee's buildings were located nearly downtown. There was another livery stable that sat on the west side of Denver, about a mile from them. It was the only other livery stable. Robert saw that the other livery stable was inconvenient for people who were downtown or lived on the eastside. He mentioned this to the group that night at supper.

The chief said, "We will need horses and carriages if we are to open our stable."

Ben said, "I think we should open it. We can all look for horses for sale. Alta, why don't you read the newspaper. See if any horses or buggies are for sale. We can all poke around, and tell people we are looking for horses. Cary and I will go to the other livery stable and ask if they want to sell any of their horses."

Sarah said, I think we could paint the coach and spruce it up, We may be able to use it as a hack for people who don't want to take their own buggies to see events."

Robert said, "That is a splendid idea. We can have a couple of uniforms made and have a footman to make a big deal out of it."

Hank said, "Barney and I can be the driver and footman. We will have to have a little help from you, Robert, on how we should act and the manners we must use."

They advertised in the paper their carriage. At the next drama at the Cow Palace, they had eight requests. Alta had bought two buggies, and using them, they were able to handle all the requests. As there were shows going on a lot of the times, they had a constant business. They were able to purchase horses and more buggies. Sarah and Alta were busy painting their new buggies a bright yellow, so they would stand out as passenger vehicles. They were constantly getting messages from the hotels to take people from place to place, especially in bad weather.

They were now bringing in a tidy income. Robert suggested to Ben to open a bank account, which he did. They were now able to purchase things they needed by simply writing a check. All their signatures were on the account, even the chief's. He said, "I bet I'm the only Indian in the West who has a bank account," which made the others smile.

The livery business was now going strong and all of them were working a full day. Alta was busy collecting the money and depositing it. She and Sarah kept the books which they did at night. They would brief all the others, once a week on their business account. Alta was a shrewd business woman, and she liked that end of the bussiness.

They had now been in Denver a year. One night Alta said, "We need to check up on Homer. I worry about him each night."

Ben said, "I'm willing to go back and check on him for you."

Alta said, "No, I must see him and the boys need to see him, also."

They then decided to plan for the trip.

Robert said, "We need to have several people stay and several go. I think we need to hire some hostlers to run the livery stable, and a couple to drive the hacks. We have enough business to pay for them."

Ben said, "I must go further east as I have buried some money back there. I also want to check my family's graves."

Cary looked at Ben and said, "I want to go where you go, Ben."

It was finally established that Alta, the two boys, the chief and Ben were to go. The number of people was for safety more than anything. Cary understood that she was needed to help run things with Robert and Sarah. They had hired three hostlers for the livery stable, all good men. Two were men out of work because of their age, mostly, and one was a young boy of sixteen whose parents had died. His name was Perry Olson and they took him into the family and changed his name to Perry Lee.

They also found men to run their taxi service. They had accumulated several buggies and had spruced them up to look elegant. The coach was still used for special events. They had bought uniforms for Barney and Hank. They both wore three cornered hats with white wigs. Their boots were black with a high sheen to them. They selected people to man the coach who were near the size of the two Dobbs boys.

They decided to take a two seated surrey that was covered. The front seat could be laid down, so that Alta could sleep on it. Barney slept with her, as it was very comfortable. The surrey would only need one horse. It was light, fast and ideal for the flat plains. It could carry all their travel needs. Ben would drive the carriage with Alta. The chief, Hank and Barney would scout. They all knew the drill, if dust from a war party was spotted. If that happened, Ben would tend to the horses, and the rest would get into position to stave off an attack.

It was late October when they left. There was a chill in the air and all were in great spirits. Ben had bought each an eider stuffed coat that had a canvas cover on the outside and a wool covering on the inside. It would shed water and was really good in cold weather. They were packed now, and each had light coats.

Cary was in tears when they were gone. Sarah said, "You love him, don't you?"

"Yes, I want to marry him, but he says we're too young. He's nearly fifteen and I'm sixteen, is that too young?"

Robert said, "By the world's standards it is, but Ben is an adult in every sense of the word. I for one will encourage him to marry you when he returns." Cary immediately rose and hugged his neck.

Sarah said, "I'm not too young to be married, Robert."

He smiled and said, "I guess we will have a double wedding," and Sarah came into his arms and kissed him.

***

They camped the first night on a small stream that they had camped when coming to Denver. Everyone knew just what to do, and in minutes there was coffee boiling and the horses staked. They were gone at dawn the next morning, and made it to the village on the Arkansas river. They decided to stay on the outskirts in a place that had been used by many campers before. They needed supplies so Ben and Hank went into the village. They passed a saloon and a man was lying on the ground just off the boardwalk. He was dressed in a suit, but it was dirty from the dust covered street.

They stopped to look at him. A man lounging against a post that held up the cover of the boardwalk said, "That's Doc Samuels. He got thrown out by Ernie Thompson, the barkeep. Doc couldn't find the money for his drink. He gets drunk every night. He's no good as a doctor, because he's drunk all the time."

Hank and Ben helped the doctor to his feet. Ben asked the man where the doctor lived.

The man pointed to a small house cattycornered from the saloon. They took him there. The house was unlocked. It had a bath tub and as Ben ran the water, Hank undressed him. They put him in the water and as the water was cold, the doctor came awake.

He said, "Who are you, and why am I in this tub?"

Ben continued washing him and said, "You were in the street with dirt all over you. We took you home and are now cleaning you."

The doctor closed his eyes and just leaned forward as Ben washed his hair. Hank had to help Ben take him out of the tub, because the doctor was unable to navigate the sides of the tub. They dried him and helped him on with some underwear and started to put him to bed. However, the bed was filthy. Ben found some clean sheets and they made his bed and changed the pillowslip. They then put him to bed and he was immediately asleep.

Ben looked at Hank and said, "How old do you think he is?"

"Not forty, but you can't tell as he's a hopeless alcoholic. He may be in his early thirties or late twenties.

"I would like to take him along to dry him out, but he would be a liability to us in a hostile land."

Hank nodded and said, "We will tend to him on our way back. He may protest, but this man needs some help."

After getting supplies, they went back to their camp. Ben told them about finding Doctor Samuels, and that he was a hopeless alcoholic. Hank suggested that they pick him up on the way back as he may be too much of a liability in hostile territory.

The chief said, "I think we should take him, now. He may be dead before we return. I worked with a missionary at the reservation. He had been sent there as we had many drunk Indians. This was the missionary's expertise. He had worked in an alcoholic's ward in Boston. He said that treatment must start as soon as possible. He also said that alcoholics could not be taken off the bottle all at once. You must gradually taper them off, otherwise, they get sick, and can't hold anything on their stomachs. I think we should take him with us. What better place for him, than on the prairie where the only alcohol available, is from us? We can give him what he needs to have."

Alta said, "I think the chief's right. We must take him. We can keep him on the backseat as the space between the front seat is filled with sleeping gear and he can rest there. What do the rest of you say?"

Barney said, "If we can help him, then we should. The chief has the expertise, so I say we take him." The rest agreed.

The next morning they packed up and went by the doctor's house and Ben and Barney picked him up, and put him in the back of the carriage. They put his pillow under his head and a blanket over him. He never woke.

They had been on the trail for over two hours when he awoke. He said, "Where am I?"

Alta said you are on the Kansas prairie going east. You are with friends who want to help you."

He said, "I don't want your help, I want a drink."

They were coming to a stream, and were stopping to water the horses. The chief made a fire, while Alta made coffee."

The chief addressed the doctor, who was now out of the buggy and by the fire, "We will give you some whiskey in your coffee, but you must eat something or we will not give you the whiskey."

The doctor was lucid enough to know, he must do what they said or he would have no whiskey. He ate some bread and meat that Alta had fixed him. The chief had taken a cup of coffee behind the surrey and put two ounces of Whiskey in it. He then walked around to the doctor and said, "Now just sip this and make it last, as you will not get anymore drink until noon."

The doctor looked up at the chief and said, "Thank, you man, my hands are shaken like an aspen."

He sipped his coffee and a look of satisfaction came across his face. He then said to Ben, "I remember you. You gave me a bath last night and put me to bed. Why would you bother with a drunk like me?"

Ben said, "Because we work for the Lord. We want to bring you into our family and make a new man of you."

He said, "But why?" Then he looked around at all of them and they all wore smiles.

They traveled on and just a half hour later, the doctor said, "I need a drink. My hands are shaking and my stomach is turning over."

Alta turned around and said, I'll help you through this, Doctor, and she climbed over the seat and sat beside him. He was shaking, and she took him in her arms like she would a baby. He clung onto her and started crying. Alta cried with him and said, "It's alright, Baby, I'm right here with you, and we'll see you through this. He cried harder and Alta cried with him. He could feel her tears running on to his head and he clung to her like a baby to his mother. It was so poignant that tears ran down Ben's cheeks. The doctor quieted some after a bit, and said, "You held me like my mother used to hold me when bad times came. She cried with me like you did. I remember when mother cried with me and held me so, that I never loved anyone so much. No one came close to the love I felt for my mother. It was like our souls touched. You gave me that feeling. For a minute or so, I thought you were my mother. Thank you. You have great compassion. Are these all your children?"

"In a sense, they are. I love each of them as I do my two boys out there," and she pointed. "Ben got us all together along with the chief. You must mind the chief as if he were your father. He has expertise in tending to alcoholics."

"Is he a doctor?"

"In a sense he is. He knows what you need, as he has tended to many alcoholics. The Indian people have a penchant for drink, and are soon addicted to it. He tended many of them while they dried out. Listen to him, and he will make it easy on you. Do you know why you drink?"

"Yes, it was the war. I was a surgeon and cut so many legs and arms off that I soon could not stand it. I watched hundreds of men die. At the last of the war, I started drinking as it would stop the nightmares I had at night. Soon, I was a hopeless drunk, and they kicked me out of the Army about the time the war ended.

"I came west to lose myself among people I didn't know. I tried to quit a million times. I knew it was killing me, but when I drank to oblivion, I had no nightmares. Soon, I had no friends. I had money and I bought a house back there and stayed in the saloon most of the day and night. Do you think the chief can cure me?"

"No, it will be Jesus Christ who cures you. No one else can do that for you. Listen to the chief, he is an educated man and knows what you need. He is also a disciple of Jesus."

They stopped for lunch and by this time the doctor hands were shaking terribly. They made coffee and the chief handed him a cup with two ounces of whiskey in it. He said, "Eat your food and sip your coffee. You need the nourishment. It will settle your stomach and the whiskey will settle you down."

That night the chief made a bedroll for the doctor. It was next to his bedroll near the fire. The chief watched him carefully all night. When the chief could see him having a nightmare, he would rub his head and whisper the promises that Jesus made, into the doctor's ear as he rubbed his head.

After awhile, the doctor's hand came over the chief's hand, and patted it as he realized he was not alone, anymore.

They were now within ten miles of Homer's farm. Hank had been watching dust to the south of them. He said, "I think that's a band of Sioux… eight to twelve of them. They must have cut our trail and are now trying to catch up to us. I figure they will hit us in another hour. We can't make it home by then. We'll have to find a place to make a stand."

The chief and Barney galloped up and shouted, "There's a creek about a quarter of a mile ahead. We need to get there, before we're attacked. There are a group of rocks there that will give us, and the horses, some shelter. Let's ride."

Ben whipped the horses and got them in a fast lope. He followed the chief and minutes later they were at the creek. There was a bank on the west side of over five feet and space enough for the horses, however, there was no cover from the creek's side. This worried them. The creek there had another bank of about five feet but no space as the creek ran against that bank.

Ben unhitched the carriage and put it against the edge of the creek bank shielding the horses. Hank said, "I think we can defend the creek side behind the carriage. I think we have a pretty defendable position, so let 'em come."

Hank began telling the others where they should defend. They now had a pretty fair defensive position. Ben was unhitching the team as Barney was unsaddling the horses. They set the saddles across the carriage for a better shield. While they were doing this, the chief and Hank made a temporary corral on each end of the space with their roped around some boulders. While this was going on, the doctor and Alta were picking up firewood and buffalo chips, and now had a fire going. Alta was making coffee while the doctor filled up the canteens.

Hank then designated places for each one of them to shoot from, giving them a defendable position. About a half-hour later, the attack came. The Indians came riding toward them with their horses at full speed. They did not aim for the Indians, they shot their horses. The chief had told them to aim at the horses. Four horses went down throwing their riders. Some of them limped away, and some were shot trying to get away. None of the Indian's horses reached their defense position.

The Indians broke off their attack and were gone. The chief said, "They'll be back as soon as they regroup. Is anyone hurt?"

No one said anything. While the attack was going on, the doctor noted that Alta was at a station with her rifle. He thought he must do something, so he made sandwiches and the coffee was boiling. When the Indians drew back, Ben said, "I'll watch, you can all get some grub and coffee. As he stood watching, the doctor brought him a cup of coffee.

The doctor said, "Although I was scared, this was the most exhilarating experience of my life. You people are better than any army unit. You all seem to know just what you must do."

Barney said, "We've been through it before. We have a man who rode with us going to Denver who was a cavalry officer. He laid out a plan that we now follow."

"Why isn't he with you?"

"He's back in Denver with two others, managing our businesses there, You see Doctor, we're a family. We call it a *Ghost Tribe*, as the chief and Ben were the first members. They had formed a family, then mother, our older sister, Sarah, and Hank joined the family. Being the chief was an Indian, we called it a tribe.

"We're on our way to our farm to check on our, dad, Homer. We have quite an investment back there, so he stayed to defend it."

"How could one man defend a farm?"

"You'll see when you meet, dad. He's an outstanding man. I think he can defend it, but we wanted to make sure, because of mother."

"That is one fine woman. I think I love her. She is so kind with me that I want to keep sober, because she wants me to."

That night the doctor asked the chief to tell him about his life. The doctor wanted to know how an Indian could be so compassionate and so articulate.

The chief said, "It was my upbringing. I was taken in by the missionaries and they taught me for nine years. I met a young woman and we married and had two children. Later a Kiowa tribe overran us and killed my two children and took my wife. I then ran with renegade Sioux that killed and plundered. When they found I would not kill they kicked me out. I went back to the mission and found new missionaries. I met a missionary who was a true believer. He was astounded at my understanding of the Bible. We discussed it many hours. At night I would think of my wife, and where she may be. I grieved for my children, also.

"The food at the reservation dried up and the young warriors left. I thought I had better go with them to try to calm them before they started doing terrible things. I went on their raids and tended the horses. We raided a Kiowa village and I went with the warriors this time to try and find my wife.

"I found her, but she was very sick. I took her back to the reservation and stole many horses. I learned to move like a ghost. She got some better, but died that year. I was happy for her as her last words were, 'I go to be with Jesus, now.' She smiled and the Great Spirit took her.

"I went back to the renegade warriors. They were glad to see me as they all realized that I was not only good with the horses, but a master stealer of horses. But, once again there was a warrior who didn't like me. He thought I was too soft. He's the one who took my horse from me when Ben found me. I had given up hope, and only wished to be with my wife again. However, the family gave me new hope."

The next morning, the chief gave the doctor only one ounce of whiskey in his coffee. He didn't complain, but knew the chief had shorted him on the whiskey. They reached the farm by mid-morning. It looked abandoned. All the livestock was gone and although all structures were empty, nothing had been taken and coffee was on the stove, although cold.

They were in the house warming the coffee when Homer came in the door. Before a word was said, Alta flew across the room and into his arms. They stayed that way for awhile and everyone could see the love they had for one another. After they parted, Homer said, "I've moved all the animals into a cave I discovered. The old timer told me about it, but I didn't explore it until the morning all of you left.

"After we have our coffee, I'll show it to you. How have you been?"

Alta brought him up to date about Denver and her sister's family dying. She then explained about their integration into the tribe and the business they had created. Homer was impressed. They later were shown the cave and were impressed.

Later Homer showed his defense system and they all liked it.

Chapter 6

BEN'S TRIP

The next morning Ben said, "I'll be back in a couple of days. I need to go and find some money I buried."

Hank said, "Barney and I will come with you."

Ben said, "No, Hank, I think it will be safer if I just go by myself. One horse makes little dust. I will watch for the Sioux, they always create dust when they travel, so I will just watch and take the necessary steps to avoid them."

He picked out a good horse, a line back dun, and packed up and left the next morning. They were sitting around having coffee and the chief said, "I'll follow him. It's no good to be alone in the plains. I'll keep behind him, but if trouble comes, I can help. I know these plains, well. I know where the water holes are, and how to live off the land. I don't think Ben has that knowledge."

Homer said, "I think you're right, Chief. I have a horse that is really good on the plains."

The chief said, "No, I have a good horse, and it was raised on the plains, so it knows things that other horses don't. I'll stay behind Ben, and he won't know I'm there, unless he has trouble."

They outfitted the chief, and he was on his way.

Ben rode that day and found a creek around nightfall. The creek had a bank that had an overhang that would shield him from the wind that had come up. He ground hitched his horse, so he could graze along the creek. There was nice grass there. He built a small fire, and cooked some bacon and warmed some beans he had brought. He always had jerky, but kept it for emergencies.

He cleaned his rifle and the handgun Hank had made him take. Hank said, "A rifle can get broken or foul up sometimes. You need to have a back up."

Ben said, "Hank, I've never fired a handgun." So, Hank went over how to fire it. He said, "First pull back the hammer with your thumb and point it like you would your finger, squeeze the trigger, and that's it. Keep this leather thong over the hammer when you ride, so if you are thrown or have to leave your horse in a hurry, it won't get lost."

As he sat cleaning the pistol, he thought of Hank and his instructions. The next day he was on his way again. He had traveled a long way this day, and the going was easy, and the dun was a fast walker.

Late that evening he saw the area where the wagon train had been attacked. It looked much different. There were graves for the people who had been killed and crosses over the graves. He could tell it had been the army, as the crosses were like those carried by the army. The wagons were gone except for a pile of the scraps. Ben could tell that a number of them had been repaired and were now gone.

Ben found his folks grave and it had an army cross on it. He stood with his hat off and wept. He remembered his father, mother and his sweet sisters. He then went to the boulder. Nearby he had hidden a shovel in a crack between two boulders and retrieved it and began to dig. He soon had the iron box on top of the ground where he emptied about half its contents into his saddle bags. The saddlebags were heavy to lift and he wondered how this would affect his horse. He took all the paper money and some of the gold coins and put most of the gold,silver, watches and rings back in the iron box and reburied it. He lifted his saddle bags again and they weren't nearly as heavy. After reburying the iron box, he hid the shovel again.

After he had eaten, he found a place to sleep and within minutes was asleep. He was wakened by the light. The sun wasn't up, but he rose and shook out his shoes and was now dressed. He saddled his horse, then put the saddle bags on and he was away.

He traveled a far piece that day, but toward sundown saw dust. He watched for awhile, and the dust seemed to be coming straight for him. He went north to avoid them, but thought, "*They will see my tracks. I had better look for someplace to make a stand. When night comes, I will slip away.*"

Ben found a buffalo wallow. It was only three or four feet deep. It had a juniper growing that was about twelve feet tall. His mind was turning on what to do. He saw where an animal had started a borrow and then abandoned it. It was some two feet deep. He thought how much the gold weighed and decided he would bury the saddlebags with the gold there.

He threw the bags into the hole and then used his hands to push the dirt back to cover the hole. He stomped down the dirt and put more in. He then looked for some rocks to put over the hole to make the ground look natural.

He thought, "*I can't take the horse if I slip away. They would soon ride me down. I will take his bridal off so if I find another horse I can use it.*" He then thought of something else as he looked at the juniper branches. He thought, *"If I wrap some of the branches with my blanket around the juniper I cut, then tie this to my saddle, it will look like someone is riding.* He immediately went to this task. Using rawhide strips, he tied the dummy to the horse. He made it secure, so he knew it would not fall off. He put all the jerky he had in his coat pockets and the extra ammunition for his colt. He had decided not to take his rifle as it was just added weight and he needed to travel fast.

He decided to send the dun west and he would go east. If he could reach the river, they had followed from Hayes, he might make it back to there, and be safe. It was a long way, but he knew it was the only way.

Ben could hear quail calls and knew it was not a quail. He now knew that the Indians had located him and he was surrounded. It was now two hours after the sun had set and was completely dark as the moon had not risen yet. He put the bridal around his neck, put his rifle in the sleeve of the saddle. As he looked at the dummy, he decided to put his hat on top to make it to look more authentic. He tied the hat to the top of the juniper so that it would not come off. He then slapped the dun on the rear and fired his pistol twice.

The dun bolted from the wallow and in doing so, met an Indian running into the wallow. The dun hit him so hard it broke the Indian's neck and he fell into the wallow. As the dun bolted several cries went up from the Indians, and they started pursing the dun.

He heard two Indians pass the wallow running at full tilt. They were running back to where their horses were tethered. What they didn't know was that the young brave holding the tether, was looking towards where the shots had come from. He didn't see the chief slip up behind him. He hit him with the but of his rifle. The chief had then taken the tether and led the horses at a run chasing the sound of the dun running.

The Indians in front of the dun saw the rider clearly and shot at him. One of the braves was close and knew he had hit the rider, but the rider paid him no mine and bolted on. The warriors returned to their ponies, but they were gone. All that was there was the boy who was hit. He was now sitting up and rubbing his head. Several of the braves cursed him. They could all hear faintly the sound of the horses hooves as they hit the dry pack of the desert prairie, and then that too was gone.

When Ben saw the Indian who was in the wallow, there was no doubt that his neck was broken as his head was at a terrible angle. He stared at the moccasins that were on the dead Indian. He was also wearing a buckskin shirt. The Indians hat was laying beside him. It was a blue, officer's campaign hat.

Ben quickly pulled off the buckskin shirt the brave was wearing and his moccasins. He removed his own shoes. He tied the strings together and hung them around his neck. He then donned the buckskin shirt over his coat, then put on the moccasins and hat. He was now up and running east. He heard the shots that were somewhere west of him and smiled. However, he knew he didn't have much time as the Indians would now be gathering their horses. He hoped that they would ride west chasing his horse. He could hear the hooves of many horses chasing the dun. It puzzled him as he knew that they couldn't have been that fast in retrieving their horses. Maybe there were more Indians than he thought.

He was not that curious, because he knew he had to cover a lot of ground. He thought that the moccasins would make much less of a trail to follow, and that maybe they would think he was another Indian.

He would walk a hundred yards at a fast walk then run a hundred yards. The chief had told him this method. The chief had said, "A man can cover a lot of ground that way in a short time."

***

The chief was now on the trail of the dun leading eight horses and surely wasn't gaining ground on the dun. He slowed the horses to a fast trot and kept moving. It was mid-morning when the saw the dun at a creek drinking. He walked the ponies then, as they all needed rest and water. He let them drink.

He smiled when he saw the juniper branches wrapped in the blanket wearing Ben's hat. There were several bullet holes in the blanket. The chief shook his head in admiration of Ben. He waited an hour, then added the dun to his caravan and headed north. He traveled north over three miles before he turned them in a slow arc back toward the east.

He walked them now, knowing it would take the Indians until morning to trace their tracks of his caravan. In walking the horses, they would create very little dust. By that time, the chief would be too far ahead for them to trail him. They would probably head home to their village, and would know they had little hope of catching their ponies.

The chief was on hard pan now and no dust came from it, so he picked up the pace to a trot. He knew Ben was heading east and would probably be seeking refuge in Hayes. Ben had told him that it was the last town they had seen when on the wagon train before the attack that killed his folks.

The chief passed the fort that had been abandoned months ago. He didn't stop there as he wanted to reach the river that ran east to Hayes. A day later he found it. At the river he met a some raw-hiders going west, as the buffalo would be coming through the plains ahead soon. He told them about stealing the horses from the Indians and they all laughed. He sold the ponies to the raw-hiders for a hundred dollars. They also wanted the dun, but he told them about Ben's escape, and that he was trailing him. They all laughed again as they saw the bullet holes through the blanket with Ben's hat atop it. The chief didn't try to cut Ben's trail as he knew he would go to Hayes.

When the chief arrived in Hayes, he went to the livery stable to feed and water the horses. The sheriff was just coming back from tracking some rustled cattle and was in a surly mood because the thieves had eluded him.

The sheriff saw the chief with the two fine horses and said, "Where did you get those horses?"

The chief said, "I'm part owner of these horses. I'm from Denver and am meeting one of my partners here."

"The hell you are. Where's your ownership papers for them?"

"I don't have them with me, but when my partner arrives he can clear this matter up."

The sheriff drew his pistol and said, "You're under arrest for horse stealing." He seized on the idea that it would take the heat off him from losing the rustlers, if he made an arrest. The chief knew that no matter what he said, the sheriff was going to arrest him. The sheriff took him to jail. As he was walking the chief to jail, a reporter from the paper came walking up and asked about the rustlers.

The sheriff said, "I caught one of them with stolen horses, and being I couldn't bring them all in, I settled for this one."

After jailing the chief, the sheriff went over to the saloon and had a meal and beer. Many people asked him about the chase of the rustlers and he told them he brought in a horse thief, and this took the heat off him.

Later he went over to Judge Baker's office and told him he had caught a man, who looked like an Indian, with two horses and had no papers for them, so he assumed he had stolen them.

The judge said, "What evidence do you have that they were stolen?"

"Well, this Indian looking feller had them with no papers, so I assumed he had stolen them."

"Do you have papers for your horse, Sheriff?"

The sheriff was now angry and said, "I have them at my ranch."

The judge said, "How do I know that. You might have stolen that horse."

"Listen, I have a thief in jail, are you going to try him or not?"

"I'll try him, but I don't see much of a chance of convicting him on the evidence you have. It costs the county money to keep a prisoner, and he will have to have an attorney. That will cost the county more money. If you lose this case it will hurt you more than help you in the coming election."

"Go to hell," the sheriff said, and left.

As there was nothing else on the court's calendar, the trial was set for the next day.

An attorney was appointed for the chief, but he was drunk to the point that he slurred his words in court. He was so ineffective that the chief was convicted of horse stealing and sentenced to hang.

***

Ben reached the river two days after the chief had passed that point. He found an Indian with a canoe and gave him two dollars to paddle him to Hayes.

They were building a scaffold when Ben came into town. He was going to the saloon for a beer, and asked the bartender who they were hanging.

The bartender said, "An Indian came to town with two horses and didn't have papers showing that he owned them."

Ben was alerted and left his beer and walked directly to the livery stable. He asked the hostler to show him the two horses that the condemned thief rode in with. He showed them to Ben, and there stood the dun and the chief's horse. The dummy was still tied to the dun. Ben retrieved his hat and put the campaign hat on the dummy.

Ben said, "Is their a judge in town?"

The hostler said, "Yeah, the judge who sentenced him to hang is Judge Baker."

"Where's his office? Ben asked. The hostler walked to the entry and pointed to the county courthouse.

Ben went to the Judge and after a few minutes wait, was allowed to see him.

Ben said, "I'm Ben Lee from Denver, where we have the Bar Lee brand reregistered. I understand you have convicted my uncle of horse stealing. He is part owner of all our horses. How could he have been convicted?"

The judge said, "I told the sheriff the same thing, but he was sure an Indian could not have two fine horses and must have stolen them."

"How did you assume he was an Indian?"

"Well, he had dark skin."

"So anyone with dark skin is an Indian?"

"The judge said, "He was tried before a jury and found guilty.""

"I have identification that shows I'm Ben Lee, and I will swear that this man is my uncle and owns both horses in part, as we have a company that owns them. Here is my identification." It was a certificate of the registration of the brand in Denver.

The judge said, "That is what your uncle said, but he didn't have any proof."

"So the burden of proof is on the defense?"

"Stop it! you've made your point. I'll write out a "stay of execution" and a writ showing that the man is innocent."

The judge got busy and for the next ten minutes he was writing. He gave the papers to Ben and said, "Give these to the sheriff and he will release your uncle."

Ben said, "Thanks, Judge," and walked out and to the sheriff's office."

Ben entered the sheriff's office and the sheriff was signing some release papers for another man who had served his time. The man stepped aside and Ben handed the papers to the sheriff. The sheriff read them and said, "Like hell. I'm not releasing him. I'm arresting you, too."

Ben got into the gunfighters' stance like he had seen Hank do and squinted his eyes and said. "Come on, arrest me."

The sheriff then backed up a step. He had seen gunfighters in that stance before, and knew that death proceeded nearly every time.

Ben said, "I thought you said you were going to arrest me?"

"Are you threatening me?"

"Does a fifteen year old boy threaten the mighty sheriff?"

The released man thought this was real funny and said, "Wait until the boys hear about this at the saloon."

The sheriff knew even if he won the gunfight, that Ben had a witness, and he was facing a teenage boy. He said, "Well, you do have the proper papers. I'll release your uncle, but I want both of you to leave town today."

The released man said, "I think it will be you who will be leaving town, Sheriff, when the boys hear how a fifteen year old kid backed you down."

When the chief saw Ben, a huge smile came on his face. He said, "Let's get out of here Ben. This town is rotten."

Ben agreed and as they were riding out of town they stopped at a general store and replenished their grub.

By this time the released man was down at the saloon telling how a fifteen year old kid backed down the sheriff. The judge was there and said, "He cost Hayes City a lot of money as those scaffolds cost over a hundred dollars to build." Needless to say, the sheriff lost the next election and left town.

On the way back, Ben stopped at the wallow and retrieved the saddlebags with the gold in them. Ben explained the gold, and why he had buried it.

Chapter 7

CARY'S ORDEAL

Cary's father and family had traveled to Denver prior to Cary being there. He was looking for work. He happened to meet an older man who was at the same store where Mr. Elder was looking for work. The old-timer heard the storekeeper turn him down.

Mr. Elder came outside and the old-timer approached him. He said, "My name is Hirum Welder, I'm a prospector. My partner died a couple of months ago and I was heading back to a claim I have. I found a little color and the prospects look pretty good. I can't see going back there by myself as I get too lonely. Would you consider being my partner?"

"As you can see, Sir, I am broke and have a family."

"I saw them in your wagon. I'm glad you have a family and I'm glad you have a wagon. I need to stock up on groceries, and you could haul them back to my claim. I have a cabin there for your wife and children. They can live there, and I will camp out until we can add on to the cabin. I think you can come away with some gold.

"You see, my partner, Luther, died about three months ago. I got so lonely that I came to town. When I saw you, I thought I saw a good man. Having a family makes it all that much better. I would love to hear children's laughter and them running around having fun. What do you say?"

"I'll do it, but you must know I know nothing about mining."

"I didn't either until Luther taught me. You'll do just fine."

As they traveled Carl Elder said, "I want to confess something that I did that was very bad. We were starving and I could see that if I didn't do something soon, that the kids and Nelda may die. I had a fourteen year old daughter and talked it over with her. I told her that I needed to sell her, so that the family wouldn't die. She understood. She loved us so much that she went willingly. I sold her to a drummer in Cheyenne for fifty dollars. She hugged us all goodbye."

"That was a hard decision you had to make, Carl. Some men couldn't do it. I commend you for seeing the big picture. I would surely like to meet your daughter, she must be a wonderful person. I will start praying for her every night. What is her name?"

"Cary. I weep every night about her. My wife and I decided we would not mention her name again as to do so was like putting a knife in both of us."

"Carl, once we are making some good money from the claim, let's place an ad in the Cheyenne and Denver papers telling her where to contact us. We'll get her back, Carl, I promise."

Two days later they arrived at the claim. It was a beautiful place. Hirum and Luther had built a sturdy cabin on a shelf just in front of their diggings. There was a gorge just north of the mine that they dumped the waste material in. Carl did just what Hirum said. They worked a half day mining and the rest of the day they spent enlarging the cabin. As a matter of fact they more than doubled the size of the cabin. Nelda helped in the planning and the whole family helped in building it.

As they were sitting out front of the cabin after supper, Hirum said, "Do you see that shelf just north of us?" They looked and it was a shelf about seventy feet higher than where they were. "From there you can see down the valley some three to five miles. You can see every animal we own from there.

"I want to build a large home on that shelf for us. I want it to be the largest and most fancy home in Colorado. It can be seen for miles, and people will say, 'That's the Elder - Welder mansion.' I want us to sit out on the upstairs veranda and sip mint juleps as the old Southerners use to do. I want it to look just like the old mansions that were in the South before the war.

"The stables and bunkhouses will be down below. You and I will live a life of comfort. Nelda will have house servants and we will have seven or eight cowboys and run a thousand head of cattle and many horses."

Carl said, "I hope we can dig out enough gold to do that."

"Carl, I have no doubt that we will. That gold in that strata looks rich. I think we can dig out a ton of gold.

"Carl, I don't want this to sound like I don't trust Nelda, but lets tell her we have a little gold, enough to buy what we need. However, we have a lot of gold, and just one slip of the tongue, and we will have this valley swarming with gold-crazed people."

"Nelda is not much of a talker, but I see your point. As long as our bonanza is only known to us, we're safe, so I think your suggestion is wise."

They didn't get back to Denver until the spring. They had dug out over a hundred pounds of gold. They had melted their gold to get the impurities out and poured it into molds that weighed approximately five pounds. When they reached Denver, they let Nelda and the children out at a department store to buy the clothes they needed, and Hirum and Carl drove straight to the mint. The mint was delighted to buy the gold. The director told them they would assay it, and have a price for them the next day. Hirum had a bank account, but he wanted Carl's name on it, also. They dropped by the post office and got a box. They then went by the new paper's office and placed an ad that ran once a week in the Cheyenne and Denver newspapers. The ad asked that Cary Elder contact her family and put their post office box number in the ad.

They picked up Nelda and the children and took them to a boarding house. The landlady was glad to have them.

After the money was transferred to their bank, Hirum and Carl went to the land office and were able to buy the three sections of land that included their claim and the portion that ran north past the shelf, that they wanted to build on. Their property ran south three miles to Squaw Creek, which was the southern border. The western border were the mountains that were inaccessible. The eastern border was a road that ran south to a town called Green Valley. The cost of the land they bought, was five dollars an acre. However, they were able to purchase the three sections for eight thousand dollars as the land office had been informed to drop their price if a large area was asked for. It was a lot of money, but it was worth it to them.

There was a spring fed lake near the center of the property which covered five acres. A creek ran to and from the lake making it a good place for the cattle to water.

Although the three sections they bought were very distinguishable, they decided to put in corner markers. They had a land surveyor establish monuments, and record a map of their property. Both Hirum and Carl knew there were squatters that were moving in around Verdi and wanted no land ownership problems.

Hirum said, "We may ought to fence the east side so squatters would know it's private property. When we have cattle, they couldn't wander off as the other three sides have natural barriers."

While they were in Denver they contacted a man who built fences for a living. They showed him their map and got a good price from him for building a four strand bob wire fence with cedar posts. It covered the east side of their property and had a gate at the road that led east to Verdi and south to Green Valley.

As they were returning to the boarding house, Carl asked, "What about Squaw Creek, Hirum? Odom may want to drive cattle across the creek to use our pastures. Let's ask the land office to write Odom a letter showing our purchase, and showing Squaw Creek as our southern border."

Hirum said, "Odom would have to drive his cattle up the road towards Verdi to the bridge that crosses Squaw Creek. On our side of Squaw Creek there's a bluff of about thirty feet, making it inaccessible to cross, however, I think it would be wise to have the land office inform Odom about our purchase.

They went by the land office and asked the clerk to write a letter to Odom at their request, and include a map of the Elder - Welder ranch.

When Odom received the letter he was enraged. He had always thought he would build a house on that shelf, and use the land they had purchased as pasture. Odom had not purchased any of his land. He had just used his homesteaded forty acres for his home and his out buildings. He just used the government land as pasture as it was open range.

Odom wrote the land office and protested the purchase, saying that he had used that land in the past and had run cattle on it. He claimed prior rights. However, the manager of the land office wrote back saying, "Any government land can be purchased. The E and W ranch was in its right to purchase it, as only their cattle occupy it. It has been surveyed and has a recorded map now. There is nothing you can do, but try to purchase it from them."

He wrote back asking how much they paid for it.

The reply was, eight thousand dollars.

Odom was talking to his foreman, Bob Fulton and said, "How in hell could they have that kind of money?"

"They probably inherited it. People get money all kinds of ways. Look how you got your money."

Odom smiled, as he had told Bob the story of how he got the money for his ranch. He robbed a bank in Hays City, Kansas with two other men, both of whom were killed in a shootout. Odom was just lucky and got away with over six-thousand dollars.

"Bob said, "Why don't you talk to them, Mr. Odom. Most people get fed up with the loneliness, and want to sell out. You might just get it for a bargain."

"That makes sense, Bob. Let's go over there tomorrow."

Just he and Bob rode over and Hirum and Carl came out and said, "Welcome. We don't get many visitors. Why don't you get down and sit a spell."

Odom said, "We don't have much time. I'm here to make you an offer for your land and buildings. I understand you paid eight-thousand dollars for the land. I'm willing to buy it from you for ten thousand."

Hirum said, "Thanks for the offer, Mr. Odom, but Carl and I plan to spend the rest of our days here. But thanks for the offer. I hope we can work together. If you need help, just come around and ask."

Odom did not answer he just turned his horse and left. Bob stayed just a minute and said, "Otis had really counted on buying that land," then he too, turned his horse and left.

As Odom left he thought, *"I don't have much money anyway. Most of my money is tied up in the two-thousand head I'm running. It would be late summer before I have the cash to offer them. If I offer them fifteen-thousand, I'm sure they will sell. That's a lot of money. Damn it! I should have built a house up there years ago, but I was too busy stocking my herd. Oh well, they will sell, and if they don't, I will encourage them to do so. They have no hands. I'll approach them this fall."*

***

After the people were off to check on Homer, Cary was reading the newspaper as she did everyday. She was looking at the ads, and she was shocked to see the ad asking her to contact the Elder family. She immediately wrote a letter and carried it to the post office. She asked to speak to the clerk who handled the post office boxes.

He grinned and said, "You are the fourth person to answer that ad. I will put your letter with the rest in their P. O. box."

Cary now wished she had given more details. When she returned home she wrote a detailed account of each member of the family saying she wanted to see them badly and gave the address of the Lee Hotel. There was no immediate answer. She knew it would take time as her father may be working out of town. She was anxious to see them though.

***

The town just three miles east of the E and W Ranch was named Verdi, after the name of the man who built the first store. Alton Verdi encouraged others to start businesses there. It was slow starting, but after a few years, they had along with Verdi's general store, a saloon, barbershop, hotel and livery stable. Several miners had built houses, so they could winter there. The town now had about sixty permanent families living there. They were now talking about starting a school.

A man named Tollivor was the first to start a bank in Verdi. He was actually an employee of the Denver Bank. After the bank was built, the post office opened. A stage line ran from Denver to Verdi then south to Green Valley, so Verdi was getting larger.

The Odom ranch was three miles southeast of Verdi. Odom was hard on his ranch hands, but paid them well. The hands came into Verdi to the Hard Luck saloon each Saturday night. They raised a little hell, but it was confined to the saloon. The owner, Boone Hendricks, employed two girls who danced and talked to the boys.

***

The trip back to Homer's ranch was uneventful. Ben and the chief were very careful, but they made good time as their horses were the best. They had now been gone over two weeks and everyone was worried.

Hank saw them first as he was standing watch on the shelf overlooking the area. He yelled, "Riders coming!" Everyone got into their positions that Homer had drilled them on. As the riders got closer, Hank yelled, "Just two riders." All their hopes were up now, as they hoped it was Ben and the chief.

When they arrived everyone hugged them. They went inside and had coffee, while each one explained their ordeal.

Homer said, "I've made a decision. I'm going back with you. The hogs can make it on their own and we'll drive the horses and cattle back to Denver. With the dust they will turn up, I don't think we'll have any Indian trouble. Four days saw them on the outskirts of Denver.

They were all tired as they rode up to the livery stable and unsaddled and rubbed down their horses. They then went to the hotel. Sarah, Robert and Cary were elated at seeing them.

Ben could tell Cary was attracted to him. He loved her, but was surely not ready for marriage and a family. However, if that was what Cary wanted he would tell her he couldn't do it. However, she never showed that she wanted marriage at that time.

It took awhile to tell their story. Homer asked, "How will I fit into this family?"

Robert laughed and said, "Homer, there's so much work around here, you will be chasing your tail. After you get into the swing of things, you will probably be running it."

Cary then told about the ad in the paper. She said, "I am so anxious to see my dad and mother. The girls must be a head taller by now."

***

It was now fall and school would be starting soon. Nelda and Carl talked it over and decided that the kids must go to Denver to attend school. Hirum agreed. He said, "A kid needs an education these days. What are you going to do about boarding them?"

Nelda said, "I'm going to rent a house near the school and stay with them. Thanksgiving you and Carl will come to Denver and come back at Christmas. Hirum stayed home to take care of the livestock and Carl, Nelda and the kids left for Denver. They were taking a hundred and seventy pounds of gold, also. Nelda knew they had gold, but thought it just a few pounds. Hirum and Carl had built a false bottom in the wagon and left out a few pounds for Nelda to see. The way they were dressed, no one would have believed they had twenty dollars.

When they reached Denver Carl dropped them off at the boarding house and explained that he had better take the gold to the mint. He unloaded their gold. Carl was now friends with the manager, Harold Hastings. He said, "Harold, just send the check over to the Denver Bank for deposit."

He then dropped by the post office. They had five people who claimed to be Cary Elder. He kept the letters until he got to the boarding house. Nelda ripped open the letters. The third one asked about the girls and named both the children, they knew they had the right Cary. They drove to the Lee Hotel and walked in. Cary was at a desk and flew into their arms. There was much crying and hugging.

There were sofas and chairs in the lobby. Cary introduced everyone and said, "This is my new family. They saved me. The drummer had to give me up as he lost all his money in a poker game." Leaving out the other two parties that had owned her, she said, "Ben found me and brought me into his family and I have been safe ever since."

All the Lee family knew her story, and saw that she was just saving her mother and father from knowing how she had been treated. Nelda then explained that they were in Denver to put the children in school.

Ben said, "There's a school just down the street. You can stay with us here. We have the extra rooms, and all of us want to get acquainted with you and the girls."

Carl said, "I have to get back to our place as I am here to buy supplies. I have a partner who will be needing the supplies."

Cary looked at Ben and said, "Can I go with my dad, Ben? I want to see where the family lives and visit with him and meet his partner?"

"Of course Cary, you're free now, and can do just what you want to do."

Carl said, "My partner will be glad to meet you, Cary. He's some older than me, but he knows that I had to sell you. On hearing the story, he said he would pray for you each night, so he's part of our family. The children and Nelda love him. He'll love to see a young woman about the house. You'll love him as our family does. We have been able to earn a little extra and are now okay money wise."

"I can see that. Everyone is fed up. When I left you, I thought you were all going to die of starvation. I could count the ribs on mothers sides."

Nelda said, "We would have starved, too, except that you gave us a new lease on life. I know it saved the girls' lives."

Cary and Carl left the next day about mid-morning. They had spent the first two hours loading groceries.

They arrived the second day and Hirum was pleased to meet Cary. He said, "Carl told me about you, but he never said you were as pretty as this. My you are a beauty, Cary. I always wanted a family and Carl gave me one. We recorded a will with the county in Denver. Your name is on it with Nelda's, I didn't put the girls on it because I know you and Nelda will take care of them, and it would have complicated things.

Carl never gave up on finding you. He told me the sacrifice you made for the family, Cary. You are the bravest girl I ever knew, and I hold you dear for what you did for the family."

A month after Cary came, they were working in the mine and Hirum said, "Carl, Cary is a very smart girl. I think we should tell her about the mine and the money we have made. If something happened to us, she should know all about our bank account and savings. They talked to her that night and went over all the business. They told her how and when to pay the taxes on the ranch. They even wrote the bank that Cary would now be on their account. She signed her name to the card they sent and returned it.

They had explained why they didn't tell Nelda. They explained they had enough money now and would be covering up the entrance to the mine. They sealed it with rocks in the entrance to the mine. They then put a tarp around some boards and leaned them against the opening. No one could guess there was a mine there.

They had hired a Mexican to help build a huge barn with corrals and a house for he and his family. The Mexican, Eduardo Nunez, had a family with two boys in their teens. They had planted corn and hay and had a bumper crop. Hirum and Carl had bought fifty head of cows and they ranched them.

Eduardo had told Hirum that he had a ranch in Mexico, but a large landowner had bought him out. He knew he must take the offer or maybe be burned out. So he took his family and a wagon to Colorado where he had some kin. Hirum met him in Denver and after talking to him for sometime, hired him and told him that he wanted him to build a barn, corrals, and a house for himself. He paid him fifty dollars a month for the first three months then raised him to seventy, because his boys were working.

Cary went down to meet Eduardo's wife, Juanita. She found that Juanita could speak English, well. Juanita told Cary how grateful they were to Hirum and Carl. They now visited nearly everyday.

They had bought a buggy, so they could go to church in Verdi.

They told Cary about Otis B. Odom trying to buy them out. Hirum said, "Odom tried to hide it, but I could see anger in his eyes. He thanked me, and left.

Chapter 8

TROUBLE WITH ODOM

Odom had stewed about the E. and W. ranch for months now. He wanted that land. As he was talking to the crew one day he said, "I'm going to have that ranch. If you boys will stick with me, I'll give each of you a thousand dollar bonus. I aim to kill both those men. Neither will be missed. They probably have no family, so who will know. That Mexican family may know, but I will tell them that I will employ them just like Welder and Elder and if they don't like it, I will burn them out and drive them back to Mexico. I want to build a mansion on the shelf and everyone will think I own the property then. I will find their deed and have a crooked lawyer fix it so that everyone will think I bought it from them.

I can't pay you at once, but I will give each of you a hundred dollars now, and fifty extra dollars a month until you're paid off.

His foreman said, "Boss, how are you going to kill them?"

"I'm going to just ride up and gun them down. I want each one of you to fire a bullet into them. If we are asked, which is not likely, we will say they came to our place and drew on us. We will take them to the OBO and bury them. Then if anyone asks, we can take them to the graves."

A month later, Cary was busy baking some donuts for the men. When she worked at the café that Baker owned, he had shown her how to do that. He was an expert at that, as he knew the proper ingredients and temperature to make them.

Hirum wanted to go fishing at the lake that morning, but Carl begged off, as he wanted to go up on the shelf and locate where they were going to build the mansion.

Carl had brought his binoculars and after he saw where the mansion would be built, decided to look down to the lake, and see Hirum. He was surprised. He could see six horses approaching Hirum. Hirum was now facing them. They talked for awhile, then all six men shot Hirum. He could see the smoke from their guns and the noise came to him seconds later. They put Hirum on his horse and led him to the gate then south towards the OBO ranch.

Carl was shocked. He knew it was Odom and his men. No one else had a reason. He was devastated. He walked back to the cabin. On the way he decided not to tell Cary. He made up his mind that when they came to him, he would offer to sell to Odom, for a cheap price. He would say he wanted to live in Denver. He would then get Odom to ride to Denver to record the deed and while there, he would get help from the U. S. Marshal.

When he returned, Cary asked, "Did you hear those shots?"

Carl said, "Yes, it was some hunters shooting at a deer. I think Hirum went with them."

The next day Cary and Carl could hear hoof beats coming up to the cabin. Carl turned to Cary and said, "Stay out of sight, and if trouble starts, hide in the closet and put clothes over you."

Cary was watching from a window. She stood back so no one could see her. Carl said, "Odom, we've changed our minds. We have decided to sell to you at a cheap price."

Odom said, "Not as cheap as a bullet and drew his pistol. All six of them shot Carl. Cary immediately went to the closet, and pulled the clothes over her.

Odom said, "Bob, you check the house, I know there's no one there, but check it anyway. The rest of us will ride down to talk to the Mexicans. Steve you throw Elder over your saddle and take him back to the ranch. We will bury him there beside Welder."

They then rode down to the Mexican's house. Steve had left with Elder's body that could not be seen from the Mexican's house.

Eduardo was home and Odom said, "There has been a change of ownership. I will be paying you from now on. How much did Welder pay you?"

"Seventy dollars a month. The two boys are included in the payment."

Odom thought this outrageously high, but he didn't want to make waves now, so he took out his wallet and handed Eduardo seventy dollars.

Eduardo said, "This months payment is not do for another week."

Odom said, "Well, I might not get up this way for a while, so I'm just a little early."

Bob made a cursory check of the cabin and within minutes, they were all riding back to the OBO. Cary waited another half hour before she came out. She saw that all the horses were gone. However, one was back of the barn. It was Cary's horse and she had staked it out early that morning to crop the grass that grew in the shade.

An anger came up in her that she never had before. She swore that she would avenge her father and Hirum. She went down to Eduardo's house to see if any damage had been done to them. She was relieved to see Eduardo and Juanita.

Maria explained what Odom had told them.

Cary explained that they had sold out to Odom. Maria said, "What was all that gunfire?"

Cary said, "They were shooting at a rattlesnake."

Around seven that evening she hooked up her horse to the her buggy. Hirum had bought it and the horse and made it a gift to her. They used to ride to church. She drew the buggy close to the cabin. She took all her things and all the things she would need for a trip to Denver. She knew that Hirum and her father had valuables. She found a tin box that Hirum kept. She opened it, and was astounded at the amount of cash. There was over five thousand dollars.

She then found a tin box that her father and mother used. In it was the family Bible, some keepsakes and over three thousand in cash. She put both tin boxes in her buggy, along with many items she would need on her trip to Denver, such as blankets and a pillow. Once she was packed she left. It was now after ten. On the way to Verdi she began thinking of what she would do. She changed her mind about going to Denver. It may be months if ever to get the U. S. Marshal to investigate her father's and Hirum's death.

She decided to stay in Verdi and open a donut shop. She knew that everyone craved donuts. If she severed breakfast also, she may make a tidy sum. However, her main reason was to exact her revenge. She didn't know just how she would do it, but she would figure that out.

She spent the night on the west edge of town. That would be where she would build her donut shop. There was an old building there, that was boarded up. It was a building where a café had been, but had gone broke. It had a windmill with a wooden water tank and a barn. That area was fenced by a corral.

The next morning she went to the land office, and inquired about the building. The clerk said, "Yes, the owner abandoned it. If you pay the back taxes, it's yours."

Cary paid the taxes and asked, "Is there a builder in town? I want to expand the building to fit my new business."

The clerk said, "Yes, and a fine builder he is. His name is Cole Byers. I recommend him highly. By the way, what will your business be?"

"A donut shop."

"I'll be your first customer. I love donuts, but you can't find them around here. My wife doesn't know how to make them."

After acquiring Cole's address, Cary called on him. He invited her in, and introduced her to his wife. Cary then explained that she wanted to engage him to renovate the building that she had acquired. Cole listened intently at her plans. She wanted the front of the building to remain, but she wanted two bathrooms and a bedroom attached to the building.

Cole said, "Let's go examine the building, and you can show me what you want."

They left and Cary took Cole in her carriage. When they arrived, Cole said, "Miss Elder, this building was cheaply constructed, and leaks air like a sieve. I think it would be cheaper and better if I just tore down this building, and built an entire new building. I can repair the barn and the corral, but I advise you to build a new building. Do you have funds for that?"

"I do, Mr. Byers. I want you to construct a fine building. I want a plate glass window in the front, a large dining area with a public bathroom. I want a commode and wash basin in the public bathroom. Next to that bathroom, I want my own bathroom facing a bedroom behind the kitchen. I want a commode, wash basin and a four footed bathtub. That stove in the kitchen is so old that I can't use it. I want a new stove.

"I want running water, and if possible, running hot water also. Why don't I take you home and you can get started with the design. I will come over tomorrow and look at what you have designed, and we can work together. Your fee will be what you think it should be. The clerk at the land office gave you a glowing recommendation, so I know your fee will be honest."

"Thank you Miss Elder, I have some great ideas that I have always wanted to put to use. Building a new building like you want, will be a pleasure."

While Cary drove him back to his house, she said, "If we are going to be working together, I think we should use our first names. I know yours, so if you agree, call me Cary."

Cary dropped him off. When he was inside his wife said, "That woman is just too pretty, she makes me look plain."

"Don't worry about that, Mildred. You will always be my greatest love in this world. Besides she will be working here with me, as I am going to design the building. You can probably help, and the three of us will design it like it should be."

Cole worked the rest of the day designing the building. Mildred watched and commented at times. She said, "I hope to have some of those things for our house, someday."

With the fee I'm charging, we can have a bathroom inside and a four footed tub that you can soak in."

When Cary returned to her newly acquired property she decided to survey it and see if she could visualize what she wanted. The barn wasn't so bad, but she wanted it renovated and painted. The windmill still worked and the wooden tank was covered and full of water. She saw where someone had insulated the pipes running down the side of it into the ground. There was running water in the barn as well as the building.

After looking over the café, Cary agreed that it had to be removed. She then went to the hotel and acquired a room. She got a good price, as she said she would probably be there a month. She talked to the owner, Chester Martin. He said he was the mayor of Verdi.

Cary introduced herself and said, "I plan to open a donut shop on the west end of town. I will serve breakfast and some other foods, but my main thrust will be donuts."

A smile came to Chester's face and he said, "I can't decide what will be more popular, your beauty or the donuts," and they both laughed. He added, "You will be the most popular person in town. I hope you don't decide to run for mayor. I wouldn't have a chance against you."

Cary said, "I have no political ambitions. I just want to make a fair living."

"Where do you hail from, Miss Elder?"

"Denver, but I plan to be here for a good while. My father owns some land just west of here."

"Oh, you must be Carl Elder's daughter. We all think a lot of him and his partner, Hirum Welder. They both helped me in my last election. I owe them a lot."

The next day Cary was at Cole's home at eight o'clock. Mildred had coffee for her, and they all sat at the kitchen table going over the new structure.

Cole said, "We can get all our lumber from the new sawmill. They opened only a month ago as the railroad told them that they will be coming through here to Green Valley, then on south to the mines.

"I plan to make the studs in the walls out of two by sixes to make the place warmer in the winter. I can get all the sawdust I want from the mill and I will put it between the walls for insulation. I want to make that front window large, but it will be double paned to keep the cold out. It gets below zero here a lot in the winter, and your customers will come here to get warm and eat donuts. I can see you making a fortune."

Cole showed Cary a new commercial stove from a catalog that was fueled with kerosene. He also showed her a kerosene hot water tank that would provide hot water to the kitchen and her bathroom. Cary was able to order tables and chairs for the dining room and a bedroom set for her room.

Cary knew she had hired the right person, as Cole showed her ways she would save money.

Construction began the next week as the sawmill was able to deliver the lumber immediately. Cole made sure the lumber was cured, and of the highest quality. Cary worked as Coles helper. She saw to it they had storage space in a room on the back for extra flour, sugar and lard.

By spring Cary was in business and a business it was. She had customers all day long. She had asked Mildred if she would like to work for her. She said, "I will just work you six hours. I will need you at breakfast for three hours then lunch for three hours. You will be free after two in the afternoon. I will pay you seventy-five cents a day and if it works out that I need you more, it will be a dollar a day."

"Lord knows, we could use the money. What do you think, Cole?"

"If you want to do it, I'm all for it. However, neither of us work on Sunday."

"I close all day Sunday."

"Then "I'll do it. What will be my duties?"

"To wait on customers at first, but I want you to learn the whole business. Your title will be assistant manager. I want you to handle the money end, also. We will learn that together. We'll talk to the banker about setting up the books."

In just a week, Cary could see she needed more help. She hired the daughter of family who was located right behind her barn. The family had come onto hard times and had to sell all their animals, but the chickens. Cary bought three cows for them, and two pigs. She said, that if he furnished her with milk and pork, she would pay for their feed and they would own the animals. They family was very grateful.

The new girl was only fifteen. Her name was Greta. She was already filled out and was very pretty. She worked as a waitress and helped with the cooking at times. Cary taught her to smile, and bought them all uniforms to wear. Cary wore the same uniform. Later Cary hired a black lady to do the clean up and laundry. Her name was Mary. Mary had clean uniforms that were starched and ironed. They were very pretty. Cary bought twelve of them, so they would always have a fresh uniform to wear. The uniform had a white apron and was cut a little low in the front. Both Mildred and Greta had large bosoms that showed some. This really made the uniform look better.

Cary had many takeout orders, and business could not have been better. She even thought of expanding, because at times she could not fit the customers in although the dining area was thirty by twenty, with twelve tables. However, if there was no place to sit, the customers bought the donuts and went back to their homes or businesses to eat them.

Cary had purchased some binoculars when she first arrived. On Sunday evening she rode out to a place on Squaw Creek. She had found a place that she could cross the creek from the E and W ranch up against the mountains. She found a small flat spot that overlooked the Odom home place. She surveyed the property, and could see where her father and Hirum had been buried. She noticed that Odom's front gate had an arch over it that read, "OBO Ranch." It was sturdy as it had been built out of wrought iron.

A plan started to form in her mind. She remembered that she still had the knockout drops that she had taken from Baker. A devious plan started to form. She knew all of the Odom ranch hands had participated in killing her father and probably Hirum also.

She knew that Odom let his men come in on Friday and Saturday nights. He didn't let them come all at once. Cary watched and noted when the Odom hands came and went. She waited until just two of them came to town. They would generally come in about seven in the evening, and then leave about eleven at night.

She waited until the two were leaving for the ranch. When they reached Cary's place, she stepped out and said, "I have some donuts left over. Why don't you come in and have some coffee and donuts before you ride out. Tie your horses around at the side, I wouldn't want ugly rumors starting."

Bill looked at Steve and said, "Okay, we would like that. They came in and Cary served them the donuts and coffee. The coffee had the knockout drops in it. In just minutes they both had their heads down on the table.

Cary already had her horse hooked to her carriage, and pulled it to the side of her building, where she dragged the two cowboys onto her carriage. She then tied their horses to the back of her carriage. She had brought some meat along that was laced with knockout drops.

When she arrived, the dogs of the ranch came out. She threw the meat to the dogs. The dogs gobbled up the meat and fell silent. She then took the ropes off the men's saddles and tied hangman knots in the ends. She threw the ropes over the wrought iron arch and used their horses to hoist the two men up. She tied off the ropes and then tied their horses near them and rode away.

The next morning Bob walked out of the bunkhouse and noticed the men swinging under the arch. He ran to the house to get Odom. They both stood in awe looking at the two men. They lowered the men down and took them where they had buried Hirum and Carl.

The other two hands were there and helped dig the graves. No one said a thing for awhile then Bob looked at Odom and said, "What do you think happened?"

"I have no idea. The dogs didn't bark. I know it wasn't suicide. We have no known enemies. It's a mystery."

Cary wrote to Nelda and said that they were so busy with the new cattle and crops, that they could not come for Thanksgiving.

Several weeks passed and now it was Christmas. Cary knew she must tell them about the deaths. She took her carriage to Denver and said that both Hirum and her dad had disappeared. She said, "I just knew it was Odom and his crew who murdered them, but I need proof. I don't want to go to the U. S. Marshal yet as I don't have enough evidence. I want to wait until I have enough evidence to hang them. That will be when they move on to our place. I now live in Verdi and work in a café. I'll let you know when I need you."

Nothing much happened until summer. The weather was wonderful. Cary's business thrived.

She generally ate with Cole and Mildred on Sundays.

Odom didn't hire any new men and the incident of the hanging, began to wane from their minds.

Homer had written. His letter said that if she needed him he would come live on her ranch."

Cary wrote back. It read, "It's alright Homer, I live in town now and my café job pays me enough to make ends meet. Eduardo and his boys keep up the place okay. I go out there once a month to pay them and look over the place"

She went to Denver for Thanksgiving. She stayed three days then returned to Verdi. Driving back to Verdi was easy in her buggy. The trip was over steep roads, but her horse went up and down the hills very easily. She made Verdi in a day whereas it took two days in a wagon.

Chapter 9 ══════════════════════════

THE REVENGE CONTINUES

Cary went back to Denver for Christmas and New Years. Her romance with Ben had gone cool and both were fine with that. By the first of the year, Cary was still doing great in her business. She had several girls that Greta knew, who could help out when she was gone, as the business was heavy.

The winter increased her business as her café was toasty warm and nearly all the town was in there at some time of the day. Even the town council met there as it was convenient. Some of the church meetings were held there also, so Cary opened her place to them at night.

The next spring on a Friday night two other of Odom's hands came to town. As Cary had done before, she met them as they were about to ride out and invited them in for donuts and coffee.

The next morning Odom found them hanging to the arch. Bob said, "I'm leaving you Odom. It will be me hanging there next. I don't know how, but those two men we shot, must have relatives. They know who we are. I'm going to ride to Verdi, then north to the railroad that goes to California. I may even go to Oregon. I'm out of here tomorrow morning."

"I can't blame you, Bob. I'm going to sell out, and leave, too. If I were you I would go at night, so no one will see you. Good luck."

Bob took Otis' advise and left at ten that night. It was near eleven at night when he got to Verdi. Cary was closing up and just happened to see Bob riding by. She hailed him, and he turned and rode up to her. She said, "Where are you going at this time of night, Bob?"

"I'm going to California and wanted to ride at night."

"Well, come in and have a donut or two and a cup of coffee on the house. It will be a parting present to you. Tie your horse on the west side of the café. I don't want any ugly rumors started."

Bob tied his horse around to the side as Cary heated the coffee. He ate the donuts, but never finished his coffee. Odom found him swinging the next morning.

Odom was really scared now. Cary knew he had no hands, now, and must be more than scared.

He ran an ad in a weekly paper that had just started. It read that his ranch was for sell cheap.

It was now Sunday, and Cary rode out to Odom's ranch because she had read the ad. Once she reached the Green Valley road, she turned toward the Odom ranch.

She reached the gate and the dogs were barking. Odom came to the gate with his shotgun. She said, "Why the shotgun, Otis? Are you expecting trouble?"

"I've had some trouble, and all my hands have left me. I'm selling out."

"I read the ad. That's what I came to talk to you about. I came to make you an offer for your place and your herd. It will be a cash deal. Could we go up to your house and talk about it?"

"Sure, Cary. This may be a good deal for both of us."

They went to the house and discussed the price. Cary said, "I have twelve thousand dollars and that is all I can offer. I know it's below what you could get if you advertised in the Denver paper, and waited a few months, but that's my offer." She brought out the cash and laid it on his kitchen table.

Odom said, "I'll take it."

"Just sign the deed to the homestead, and make out a bill of sale for the cattle. I'll make us some coffee while you do that. Odom finished his paper work about the time Cary had the coffee ready. He drank the coffee and a few minutes later his head hit the table.

Cary went to her buggy and got some rope and tied Odom up. She then dragged him out to her buggy, and took him to the arch. She used a rope under his arms to stand him up on her buggy and tied him off so he would be standing on the end of her buggy. She then put the rope with the hangman's noose around his head. She waited until he became lucid.

He then saw the fix he was in and said, "What the hell is this?"

"It's your hanging day, Otis. I'm going to hang you. You shot my father and Hirum. I was in the cabin, and witnessed it from the window, then hid. I saw all of you shoot him. You are now going to be hanged. Do you have any last words?"

Otis began to cry and said, "Please don't hang me."

"Is that all you have to say? She took her knife and cut the rope that was under his arms holding him up. She then said, "Goodbye, Otis Odom," and drove her buggy out from under him and saw him hanging. She could tell his neck was broken, so she cut him down and took him back to the house. She spent the next two hours digging his grave, beside Bob's grave. She put a blanket around him and pushed him in it. After covering the grave she went back to the house,and picked up her money and the papers he had signed. It gave her title to his ranch and cattle. She then rode away as it was nearly dark.

After opening up the next morning she told Mildred she had some business at the ranch to take care of. Mildred said, "Don't worry, Greta has a new girl we need to break in. Is there anything else I need to do?"

There is the receipts from last week that need to go to the bank, could you handle that?"

"Sure Cary. Don't worry about a thing."

She drove her carriage out to the ranch and met with Eduardo and Maria. She said, "I have bought Odom out. I will need someone to run his ranch. I now own his herd of about a thousand head. Do you have any kin that need jobs?"

Eduardo said, "This couldn't come at a better time. We received a letter from Pueblo last week. My brother sold his pig business there, and is looking for a new job. He's had it with pigs."

"I don't blame him. Is he good with cattle?"

"Yes, but I think I would like to run the Odom place, and put my brother here. I will need several other vaqueros, but I have many cousins."

"You figure out how much to pay them. I will open up a bank account for you. After you have the men you think you need, we will sit down and work out the details of the pay. Here's a thousand dollars to get started. Your people will need moving money.

"Odom and his hands pulled out Saturday, so you will have to send Pedro over to feed the stock. He may ought to stay over there awhile until your brother arrives. By the way, the new brand will be the LOBO so it will be easy to re-brand the cattle."

"Eduardo smiled and said, "You think of everything. I can handle it, so you will have no worries."

She decided she needed to go to Denver. In Denver she went to the bank and told them that Hirum and her father had died. She would be the only one on the account now. She went to re-register Odom's brand to her brand, the LOBO. She took her deed to the county clerk and filed her deed and noted the cattle she had bought.

After two days, she had all her business taken care of. She never went by the Lee hotel and none of them knew she was in town.

When she returned to Verdi, it was after dark. She went by Cole and Mildred's house to talk to them. She said, "I want to pull out of the donut business. I would like to make you a fulltime partner Mildred. I will add your name as half owner of the café and the property I will require you to pay me half the earnings if you accept. I have bought my own ranch, and will be working that for awhile. What do you say?"

"My you have put a lot on my plate. Do you think I can handle it Cary?"

"Probably better that I do. You know everything I do, plus you know the help you will need better than I do. I just ask that you not work yourself to death. Hire more help, and just do the managing."

Mildred said, "What do you think, Cole?"

"I think you should take it, if that is what you want to do. We can then have the money to build us that house we talked about."

Cary said, "Cole, I have seen how the town is growing, and other towns around us. I would like to start a construction company. You would manage it and I would furnish the money to get started. We can workout the details later. I would want to advertise the company in the Denver newspaper and put posters up advertising our new business. I think you will need a couple of carpenters to start. You will know how to pay them. What do you think?"

"My gosh, you have turned our world upside down, Cary. This is something I've wanted to do for the last two years, but I never had the money to get started."

"How much front money will you need, Cole?"

"At least three thousand dollars. Do you have that kind of money?"

She pulled out a wad of bills from her purse and started counting out three thousand dollars. They were in awe, as they could see, she had much more than the three thousand dollars. Cary then commented, "My father and his partner were killed. They left me this money. I want to invest it in people like you and Mildred, Cole. I believe we can build an empire if we work together."

They spent the rest of the evening talking about the new business. At last, Cary went back to her room at the café and went to sleep quite happy.

**

It had now been four years since they had arrived in Denver. Robert and Sarah now had two children, and ran all their businesses through several managers that they hired.

The store to the west of them had been turned into a medical clinic. Dr. Samuels had began practicing medicine again. They had really spruced up the building inside and out and he had as many patients as he could handle. Robert had a hand in the renovation. He said, "If Dr. Samuels is to be a success, we need to remake that building so that it looks like one of those clinics back east." They all agreed.

The doctor had hired two pretty nurses who wore nurses uniforms. They had a sitting room for patients, and someone who checked the patients in. It was only a short time before patients saw that if they didn't want to wait an hour or two, they had to have an appointment.

Sarah suggested they run an ad in the Denver Post telling about Doctor Samuels. He was handsome, so they ran his picture with the ad. His name began to circulate in Denver's society, and he was invited to all the social events. He attended very few as between his clinic and his church work, his time was very limited.

He brought the chief into his business as a practitioner, who treated patients with lesser problems. The chief now kept his hair cut very short and wore a white coat and looked like a doctor. Everyone had quit calling him "chief" and referred to him as Dr. Lee. He also was taken into Denver's society, as no one knew him as an Indian. His vocabulary had increased and his diction had always sounded like the missionaries from back East.

The medical clinic was one of the high points of the Lee's businesses. They had also spruced up the hotel and had put a covered boardwalk between the clinic, hotel and office for the livery stable. These three building had the look of success.

Homer had been put in charge of the livery stable and the taxi service. His mind was very invocative. He suggested that they buy out the livery stable across town so they could control the prices. He kept the prices reasonable, while still making a good profit. No one knew that both livery stables were owned by the Lee consortium.

Alta and Sarah ran the book keeping, and turned the offices of the hotel into the business offices. They had hire an educated bookkeeper from back east that revolutionized that department. His name was Winston Hampton.

Winston was very astute in running businesses. He had married a Chinese woman, and his father disowned him. They had married when he was in his late twenties and had saved their money. They moved to Denver to get a fresh start. When he first arrived, he read an ad in the Post where the Lee Company was hiring a bookkeeper.

Once he met Alta, Robert and Sarah, he and his wife, Rae Ling, knew they had found a home. After he was hired it was only a short time until they saw his acumen of bookkeeping and running businesses. Before the first year was up they had named him general manager of the Lee company and Robert worked as his assistant.

Winston suggested that they form a corporation with officers. They did this and he was elected the president, Robert the vise president, Alta the secretary and Sarah the treasurer. They began constructing buildings to the west of the medical clinic and connected them to other buildings in the heart of Denver.

The third year they built a hotel. Their hotel, was used exclusively for their living facilities. They had a fulltime cook who had an assistant. No one had time for cooking as all were busy. At mealtime they all assembled, and while eating discussed the business that each were doing.

Homer had enhanced the business of livery stable to buying and selling horses. Hank and Barney tended to that business and it turned into being one of the best businesses that they had, because people needed horses.

Hank had met a horse rancher to the south of Denver who furnished them with splendid horses. Barney and Hank became experts in this area and liked to do it. They met many people, and both had a winning personality. They had a slogan that said, "We will put you with a horse that we guarantee," and they followed up with their slogan. People trusted them, and that was half the battle in sales.

Rae Ling's mother moved to Denver. They had run a store that sold merchandise from foreign countries. She knew how to order these items and knew what people liked. Winston talked the others into building a store for her. Within six months, she had a thriving business.

Word spread that the Lee corporation would sponsor businesses. Men would get on the agenda of their weekly corporate meetings and ask to partner with the Lee corporation. These men did not have the capital to go into business, but had expertise.

The board would carefully look into these men's request and would sometimes sponsor them. They would even build a building for them, if their idea was good enough. This proved to be a great asset. Ben was put in charge of monitoring these businesses. He would come to Winston for advice when he thought he was over his head. Nearly every time Winston would say, "Ben you have a good head. Do what you think is right?"

At one of the corporate meetings, that everyone of the Lee family attended, Winston brought up the need for a lawyer. They were paying a law firm a considerable amount of money each month to keep up with their legal needs.

The chief said, "I am treating a middle-aged man who was a hopeless alcoholic. He's a very smart man. I believe we should bring him into our tribe. If we can keep him busy enough, and support him, I think we will not only salvage a good man, but help us, also.

Wilson said, "This is very interesting. Could we meet with him?"

"Sure, I will have him at the next meeting."

The chief, or now Doctor Lee, brought Martin Landry to the next meeting. Martin said, "I am an alcoholic, and will always be one, even though I now don't drink." He turned to the chief and said, "Without this man, my life would be over. He was sent by God to deliver me. I was a successful corporate lawyer in New York City, but I became an alcoholic and lost my business, my wife and children and self respect. I want to change, but I will need Doctor Lee's constant support. I can handle legal matters for you, and will only require my room and board as pay, as I could never pay Doctor Lee for what he did for me."

They had Martin wait outside as they discussed taking on Martin. Ben said, "This is why the Lee family was formed, for a man like Martin. I believe we cannot only salvage a man's life, but also enhance our business."

Alta said, "I believe you, Ben, but let's hire him on a trial basis. This way he has something to work for."

Winston was convinced and said, "May I have a motion to hire Mr. Landry on a trial basis?"

Dr. Samuels said, "As a fellow alcoholic, I move we give Mr. Landry a chance. If he fails, it will be our fault. Alta can help this man more than anyone. I think he should live in our hotel, so he gets to know us all. I suggest that he be given a room next to Alta and Homer."

The motion was passed and Martin was brought into the meeting to see all smiling at him. He knew he had been hired. Winston laid out the terms. He was to reside at the hotel and take his meals there. They would take part of the lobby and turn it into a law office. He then said, "Martin, we were all failures at one time, but by coming together we are all much stronger. I believe you can change like we all did, and become what you want to be. For spiritual guidance, you can't have a better mentor than Doctor Lee."

He then turned to Alta and said, "I want you to meet with Alta a hour each day. She will come to your office to council you. She is the mother to all of us, and will become your mother, too. You will understand that more as you get to know her.

Martin was overwhelmed, and began to cry. Each of the members came by and hugged him, especially Alta. She said, "You will become my boy, Martin. Just give God a chance to help you."

Little by little Martin changed. He now wore a business suit and handled their legal needs expertly. He was now a vital member of the Lee family.

Chapter 10

LOVE AND MINING

Ben, Dr. Samuels and the chief met once a week to study the bible. A young pastor had joined them that was fresh out of a seminary. He began leading their study and brought great insight to their study.

Ben and Chief Lee had met some missionaries at their church that were heading for Cheyenne to help in a mission for Indians. When they learned that the chief, now referred to as Doctor Lee, had worked with Indians before, and knew their language, they begged him to come with them. He finally said, "If Ben will go with me. I won't be away from Ben for any reason."

The missionaries looked at Ben with such pleading eyes, that Ben said, "It's the Lord's work, so why not. I've heard they have a business school in Cheyenne that I want to attend.

The board meeting was the next night and Ben said, "Missionaries have asked the chief and I to go with them to Cheyenne to help them with the Indians. They have no expertise on handling the drunks there. They don't speak the language or have any training in that area. As their leader put it, they just told the Load they were available. They arrived here Saturday, and we met them Sunday at church. They need the chief badly, but he won't go unless I go with him. I feel the calling, so I'm asking you to let us go."

Winston said, "If the Lord is calling, you can do no other. We'll pick up the slack. Can you do without the chief, Doctor Samuels?"

"No, but I will. I need to take on another doctor anyway, so this is forcing my hand. I agree. If the Lord is calling, then you two have no other choice. We will manage. Go with God.

***

Cary had bought Nelda and her girls, a home in the nicest neighborhood in Denver. She did this as she wanted them to go to the best high school. The two girls and Nelda was elated with the gift. Cary passed it off as some money that was left by her dad and Hirum. She also provided Nelda with a bank account that was supplied each month with three hundred dollars from her account.

She said, "Mom, dad left you this legacy. He wanted you and the girls to live comfortably. Buy the girls expensive clothes, so they feel good about themselves."

"What are you going to live on, Cary?"

"I have the donut shop in Verdi, and it pays me enough to live comfortably. I like Verdi and think it will be my home."

Homer and Alta returned to their stage station. The military had returned to the fort that was only eight miles from Homer's and Alta's stage station. With the military at the fort, there was little threat from hostile Indians. Homer now furnished the fort with beef and pork. They now made a better than good living. The stages were numerous and a telegraph line was put through along the stage trail.

Hank and Barney had decided not to go back with their folks, as they saw the way station as isolated. Homer and Alta understood the boys, and agreed that they should stay in Denver. However, the past Christmas Cary talked to both boys in private.

Cary said, "I have a mine that produces a fortune in gold. I would like you two to mine it. I would require that you tell no one about it. If you can do that, I will go on the halves with you."

"Where's it located?" Hank asked.

"I won't tell you that until you swear to secrecy."

Hank looked at Barney and said, "We've got nothing to lose. I would like another adventure."

"Sounds good to me," replied Barney.

"The mine is only about three miles from Verdi, so you can go in on the weekends and blow off a little steam. You'll have to wait until spring as the mine is in the high country. It would be hard working, as the temperature gets below zero. I'll write you when it's time to come. Besides, you both are vital to the taxi business, and it will take you some time to find some people to run that. I'm sure you'll want to clear it with the board." She smiled and said, "I see everyone has strong ties to the *Ghost Tribe* and you will have to clear it with them."

Hank said, "I don't think they'll stop us when we tell them that we have been offered a real lucrative job in a gold mine. We'll add that we won't be leaving until spring. What are you going to do while we're mining?"

"I have a donut shop in Verdi. I'll meet you there and take you out to the mine.

"I suggest that between now and then, that you get with some miners and learn a little about the trade, even if you have to pay them. When you come, bring some mining gear. The miners you meet will tell you what you need."

After Cary left, Barney said to Hank, "Let's advertise in the paper that we want to learn mining, and are willing to pay for advice. We can have them mail in their qualifications."

"That makes sense. We will interview anyone who answers our ad. We can then see if we want to hire them."

They got busy wording the ad, so they would get the proper responses. After that, they insisted that they pick up the mail at the post office.

They received three responses. They answered all three of the answers to their ad. They had each one come to the Lee Hotel at a certain time. They settled on a man who claimed to have some college work in mining, and a lot of actual experience. His name was John Reese. They paid Reese, and received their money's worth. Reese wanted to come with them, but they said, "No, we have a partner who owns the mine, and we had to swear to secrecy. The mine may not be worth a plugged nickel, but we have only a little money tied up in equipment and our time, so we'll give it a try. If we see it's over our heads, we will contact the owner and discuss using you. Thanks for your time and effort. We will keep in touch."

The next April they bought a wagon and two mules to pull it, and headed for Verdi. They met Cary at her donut shop. She explained that she didn't work there any more, but stayed there as she had her own room. She said, "If the mine pans out, I may build a house out near the mine. Dad and his partner, Hirum Welder, planned on building a home like the old plantation homes in the south if they struck it rich. So work hard. I want to build that mansion."

She went with them to the general store to pick up the food supplies they would need for a month. She knew much more about this than they did. They were both surprised when she paid for the goods.

She smiled and said, "I'll get you started. I'll be around from time to time as I run cattle on the property below the mine. You can follow me out to the mine. Remember, no one knows about the mine, so never mention it. Act like you're cowboys working for the LOBO ranch. That's my brand. I will furnish you both horses to ride into town on. They will have my brand on them, so everyone will assume you are just my cowboys."

As they were following Cary out to her ranch, Hank said, "That Cary is good looking. It seems her romance with Ben is over. I bet she doesn't even know that Ben and the chief are leaving for Cheyenne."

Both Hank and Barney were amazed that the ranch that Cary owned was only three miles from Verdi, so they arrived in less than an hour. Cary introduced them to the cousin of Eduardo, Rudi Nunez. Rudi spoke good English. He was about forty and had a large family with two teenage boys. They all had smiles on their faces when they were told that Cary had hired Hank and Barney to see if they could mine a little gold from a mine that her dad had tried to mine.

"Good luck, Senors, but I must tell you that mining is a hard business. I have done it before and few can make a living at it. However, it gives a man time to think of what he really wants to do in life. When I was mining I thought about raising cattle. I did some in Mexico, but we, like Eduardo, were run off by a large land owner."

He grinned and said, "Juanita and I will expect you for Sunday dinner."

"You can count on that Rudi," Hank said, and they departed for the cabin on the shelf.

They unloaded the supplies, then Cary showed them the mine. She said, "You will have to remove all those rocks in the entrance. Dad and Hirum had grown tired of mining and closed it up. No one can see the mine because it sits behind the cabin. You can drop the rubble off the shelf at the north end. There should be a wheelbarrow inside the mine.

Cary spent the night as she had her own room. She cooked for them that night, and they were delighted with what a fine cook she was. She also cooked the next morning. She stayed with them the first week.

They cleared the rocks away and began the mining. They were astounded at the richness of the vein they were working. After they extracted the gold and panned the leavings, she showed them the molds and the cauldron where they could melted the gold.

By the end of the week they had two five pound ingots of gold. Hank said, "Cary I can see us getting very rich if that vein continues. We're not real good at mining, yet. But give us a month or two, and we will be much better. When I first thought of mining, I looked at it as hard work, but after seeing the gold, we love the work."

Barney had gone to feed the horses and mules, as it was his turn. Hank and Cary were sitting out front drinking coffee.

Hank said, "Cary I'm beginning to like you very much."

She laughed and said, "You're falling in love with my money."

"We will all have money, Cary. I want you to stay near us. I'm at the point in life where a man should think of settling down and having a family. You're a God fearing woman, who knows a great deal about life."

"Are you proposing to me, Hank?"

"Not yet, but I am getting serious about you. Do you feel anything for me?"

"Sure. You're handsome and have good manners. You're a man nearly any woman would like. However, you don't know too much about me. I think I need to tell you about myself, then you may not see me in the same light."

"Oh, I know about your dad having to sell you, but I look upon that as a noble thing. I really admired you after Ben told me the story. He told me that it was almost a holy thing what you did for your family, and I felt the same. Do you still have feelings for, Ben?"

"Yes and no. Ben and I talked about our love. He told me my love was mostly gratitude and that his love was from loneliness. We still love one another, but more like brother and sister now. Ben is going to Cheyenne with the chief and some missionaries to minister to the Indians. He is so noble. He gave his heart and soul to Jesus and I don't think anyone has a closer walk with the Lord. So yes, I love him, but we will never marry.

"I'm glad you told me that. I think I love Ben a little more, now. I feel like you do, I love him for his walk with the Lord."

"There are other things that you need to know. It has nothing to do with love or sex. It's something I did that I must tell you about before we have a romance. I do like you, Hank. Your folks did a fine job on you and Barney. If I had a brother, I would want that brother to be Barney. He looks up to you with great admiration."

"I know. Dad pointed that out to me. He said that I have a great responsibility because Barney looks up to me. He said I must live my life as an example for Barney. That has kept me from doing many things I might have done, as I love Barney with all my heart. I want to set a good example. When I think of doing something I shouldn't, I see Pa's look as he told me that."

"I'm glad you told me that, Hank. That alone would make me love you. But like I say, I need to tell you about something I did, first. I don't have time now, but we will take a ride Sunday and I will tell you."

Barney and Hank worked hard and Cary helped them at times. Barney could tell they had a thing for one another. While they were alone, Barney said, "Hank, I think Cary is beginning to love you. She's a fine woman. I hope you marry her."

"Why would you say that, Barney?"

"It's something I feel. I almost love her too, because I think she loves you. That alone would make me love her."

"Barney, you're the best brother in the world. Pa always said you had a love in your heart that was pure. I believe it. By the way, did you see how those sisters of Cary's are getting to be grown. Debbie almost looks like a woman."

"If she is anything like Cary, I want her. I'll look in on her when we go back to Denver." They could hear Cary coming and quit talking.

On Sunday, Cary and Hank went for a ride. They went to the LOBO ranch and Cary introduced Hank to Eduardo and Maria. She said, "Hank and his brother are doing some mining for me."

Eduardo laughed and said, "Pretty soon all the people in Colorado will be working for her, but a better boss can't be found. She pays me and my cousins too much. We make more that any other vaqueros I know of."

"You and your cousin are not vaqueros, Eduardo, you are managers of ranches. When you have the responsibility of a ranch, you deserve a manager's pay."

Eduardo looked at Hank and said, "I bet you think she is overpaying you, Hank."

"That she is, Eduardo. My brother and I are making more than we ever did before."

Cary said, "I want to show you where my father is buried, Hank." They rode over to a graveyard. None of the graves had markers, but you could tell they were graves.

Cary said, "I want to get a stone monument for dad and Hirum. They were both fine men and should have a gravestone. I may even get markers for the others."

"Who are the others?" as he pointed to the other six graves."

"That is what I want to tell you about. I will ask that you never tell a living soul, not even Barney."

Hank nodded and she continued. "Those are all the Odom ranch hands and owner. I witnessed each of these men, as they shot my father. Everyone shot. I didn't see it, but I think they did the same to Hirum. Dad tried to sell Odom the ranch, but he just laughed at him and pulled his gun. When he pulled, the rest of them did, also. They shot him down in cold blood.

"I knew the U. S. Marshal would do nothing about it, because it was my word against six of theirs. However, I devised a plan to get them hung. I hung every one of them. Before I hung Odom, I offered to buy his homestead and cattle. He sold them to me for twelve thousand dollars. He signed the deeds over to me and then I hung him."

"How could you over power men twice your size?"

"The first two were riding out of town late at night. Just as they passed my place. I called to them and invited them in for coffee. I used knockout drops on them that I had acquired from a café owner who bought me. I then dragged them to my carriage, tied their horses to the back and took them out to the Odom ranch. Did you notice that iron arch over the gate as we rode in." Hank nodded and Cary said, "I threw the ropes from their saddles through the arch and used their horses to raise them off the ground. It took a few months between hangings, but I hung all of Odom's cowhands. While he was making out the papers and signing the deeds I made him coffee with the drops in them and hung him, also."

Hank said, "How do you feel about what you did, Cary."

"I feel justice has been done. The Bible teaches that murderers should be put to death. In my case, I did just what a court would have done if they knew the facts. However, there was no way that would happen, unless I did it. I'm not proud of what I did, but neither am I sorry. Those men deserved to die."

"So now you own two ranches, and a lot of cattle, plus a mine that is worth three or four times everything you own. You are a very rich woman."

"I want to know if this changes what you think about me, Hank. If you can't live with that, we will just end it now."

"No, I still love you Cary and can understand what you did. We are all charged with doing justice, and what you did was justice. Didn't anyone ever ask you about Odom?"

"Yes and I told them the truth. He sold his ranch to me and left."

Hank smiled and said, "He went on a long trip and isn't coming back."

"Let's get married, Cary, at Christmas. Ben and the chief will be back and my folks will want to be there."

"That's a good time, Hank. I think we'll be happy. Do you remember that shelf that is north of the mine? The one that is about seventy feet above our cabin?"

"Yes."

"I told you Dad's and Hirum's dream about living there in a Southern plantation mansion. I want to build that mansion. You can see all our property from there. It will be a splendid place to live. You can see the lights of Verdi and Green Valley from their also."

"It's a great idea, Cary, but we have to dig out a lot more gold, before we can do that."

"No, I have over a half a million dollars from what Hirum and Dad took out. Mother has no idea about the money. Hirum and dad only put my name on it as he knew mother may slip, and tell someone. If she did that, there would be thousands of people coming here.

"I bought mother a nice house and pay her three hundred a month. It's more than she could ever spend on herself and my sisters. So they are fixed for life."

"Speaking of your sisters, Barney said he was interested in Debbie. He could tell I was in love with you and said if I married you, he wanted to marry Debbie."

"He doesn't even know Debbie very well."

"He said that if she was anything like you, he wanted to marry her."

"Well, she is like me, without the viciousness. I hope that is out of my system, now. I have prayed many times about what I did, and have peace with it now.

"Besides my donut shop, I have founded a construction company. Mildred is now half-owner of my donut shop and runs that. I get half the net profit from that. Mildred's husband, Cole, and I have formed a construction company. I financed the startup and had a large building and construction yard erected. We share in the expenses and he pays me half the net profit from that. So you see, Hank we'll be rich. All the towns are growing and will need buildings built."

"All I know is Barney and I have a lot of gold to dig out before we marry."

Cary's mother wrote and asked her to come to Denver as she was ill. Cary left immediately. Before she left, Hank said, "Buy yourself a huge diamond engagement ring and tell everyone we are getting married."

When Cary arrived, Nelda, was crippled with arthritis. She was not sick, but she could hardly get around. Cary took over seeing to the girls, and doing all the house work. She told Debbie what Barney had told her about liking her."

A huge smile came to Debbie's face and she said, "It's strange. I've been thinking about him a lot lately. It must be karma."

Chapter 11

LAW AND ORDER

Hank and Barney liked to go into Verdi on Saturday evening just to see some people. They liked to go to the saloon and drink a couple of beers. They would then go to the donut shop, that Mildred had turned into a regular café, and have supper. She still sold as many donuts, but other food was wanted, and there was no other café in town.

One evening as they were eating dinner, the mayor came in and sat by them. He told them about a man who was at the saloon that was a gunfighter. They had no law and this guy tried to intimidate everyone. The mayor said, "We need a town marshal to keep this kind of men out of Verdi."

Hank said, "I see a killing if we get a marshal, and we don't want that."

"Well, it might come to that. Some of those miners won't take anything from anyone, and might get themselves killed."

As they were riding home, Barney said, "Why don't you take the job as town marshal. They will only need you on Saturday night."

"One reason why I won't take it is that I want to stay alive. Marshals have a way of getting themselves killed. No, I won't take any job that would endanger my life. Remember, I'm getting married at Christmas and we have a lot of gold to dig out by then.

Barney had a derringer that he kept in a small scabbard strapped to his left hip. You couldn't see it, because of his coat. He also wore a forty-four Colt that he wore in a scabbard on his right side.

Hank asked him why he wore his gun on the right side, as he knew he was left handed. Barney said, "While they are looking at my right hand I can draw my derringer and maybe have a chance if I'm ever called out. Most men who are gunfighters wear their gun tied down low to their leg, so there is no wasted motion in their draw, but I wear my Colt high on my hip to let people know I'm no gunfighter."

Hank wore his tied down and was very fast and accurate. He never wanted trouble and would go to nearly any length to keep out of it.

The very next Saturday they went to the saloon. They were having a beer when the gunfighter, Abel Collins came in. When he came up to the bar, everyone moved down and away from him. He turned to the man to his left and said, "Get further down the bar, you stink like most of you cow handling trash." No one answered him.

To Hanks surprise Barney walked over beside the gunfighter and said, "I'll bet you fifty dollars I can outdraw you, stranger."

Collins looked at how Barney carried his Colt high on his hip with a leather thong over the hammer. He said, "You have yourself a bet."

Barney laid down fifty dollars and as Collins was putting his fifty on the counter, while watching Barneys right hand. Barney drew his derringer and had it cocked not three inches from Collin's forehead.

With his right hand he picked up the money and said, "See, you're not so fast. He kept the derringer pointed at Collins forehead and said, "I don't want to ever see you in this bar again."

Barney then took his beer and threw it on the crouch of Collins. He then said, "See, he's so sacred he peed his pants." Not many had seen Barney throw his beer on Collins and all laughed as Barney backed Collins backwards out of the bar.

Unbeknown to everyone, Hank had left the bar and was standing across the street from the saloon with his pistol out.

When Collins was outside, he shouted back, "You have to come out sometime, sucker, and I will be waiting."

Hank was behind him and said, "But if you draw that gun, I'll shoot you in the back of the head. I suggest you get on your horse and ride out of here and never come back. If I ever see you again, I'll kill you on sight. You won't even see it coming. We don't like people like you around here. I'm going to get an ordnance passed by the town council that will give any citizen of Verdi the right to kill you if you are ever seen in Verdi again."

"Who are you?"

"I'm probably the man who'll kill you if you ride this way again." Collins then got on his horse and rode east toward Denver.

Many people had come to the door of the saloon and heard what Hank told Collins. One of them was the mayor. He said, "Hank please take the job as town marshal. You won't be required to do anything, but help take care of people like Collins. You'll then have a badge that will give you the right to put people like Collins in jail."

"We don't have a jail, Mayor."

We will have. At the next council meeting I will ask for a special tax to construct a marshal's office and jail. I will also ask that you be appointed town marshal with no duties attached. I will ask that you earn thirty dollars a month."

"I'll take the job, Mayor, but put the thirty dollars a month as my part of the construction."

"Thanks Hank. We'll appoint Barney as your deputy, to back you up. I can see this town will be safer now. Come on down to the donut shop and I'll treat you and Barney to a couple of donuts and a cup of coffee. I swear that Mildred makes the best coffee I ever tasted."

While they were eating their donuts, the mayor said, "I'll also get that ordinance passed giving anyone in Verdi the right to gun down Collins if he comes back."

Barney and Hank dug gold twelve hours a day. They enjoyed doing it. Barney said, "I've never done anything that I like better than digging for gold."

Hank smiled and said, "It's the greed in us, Barney," and they both laughed.

About the last of August the mayor rode out to their cabin. Barney and Hank had just cleaned up and were drinking a cup of coffee outside where they kept some chairs.

The mayor said, "We've got some trouble, Hank. Two men are at the saloon. They killed a miner, named Kilgore, and have shot up the bar some. Everyone is scared of them. Would you come and see if you can do something about them?"

"Okay. Get the shotgun Barney."

When they arrived at the saloon, they could see through the door of the saloon. The two men were making a man dance as they shot at his feet. When the men started to reload, Hank and Barney stepped in with their shotguns aimed at them. Both Barney and Hank were wearing stars on their shirt. Both had the shotguns pointed at the men. Hank said, "Drop you gun belts or die where you stand."

The men were startled. They could see if they tried anything that they were dead meat, so they unbuckled their gun belts and let them hit the floor.

Hank then said, "Get a head of us Barney and get the jail open. Hank got in behind the men and soon they were in jail."

When they were in jail, one of them said, "You won't keep us here, we have a gang who will burn this town down if anything happens to us."

Barney said, "That may be true. But if they are not here by next week it won't matter to you. You killed Jack Kilgore, and he was well liked. I'll see you on a scaffold by this time next week. You will just disappear."

Just like Barney said, A trial was set four days hence, and they were sentenced to hang. They didn't build a scaffold, they just used a tree that had a limb some ten feet off the ground. They put them in a wagon with them standing up with nooses around their necks. The wagon was driven off and they were hanged. They were the first to be buried in a place that was designated as "boot hill."

The town was fearful of a gang coming, but it never arrived. The bartender was asked by a man if he had heard of the Brown brothers. He said, "Yes, they were in here about a month ago. They got mad at one another and shot it out. They killed each other and we buried them on boot hill. There is no marker on their graves."

That was all they ever heard of the Brown gang.

***

Christmas came and Barney and Hank loaded up there gold and took it to the mint in Denver. Barney's end was over a hundred-thousand dollars. The boys had sealed up the mine entrance as Hirum and Carl had done. The entrance looked like Carl and Hirum had left it. Both thought they had enough, and knew they could come aback anytime if they needed money.

Barney met Debbie, who was about to graduate from high school. They were together a lot, now. Cary and Hank were married. Ben, and the chief were there for the wedding as was Homer and Alta.

Homer and Alta had a young couple living at the stage station now, so they could get away now and then.

Cary and Hank decided that they would have their honeymoon in Denver. While there, they engaged an architect to build the mansion they wanted. The architect drove out in his buggy with two other men to take measurement and to locate where the mansion should be.

Barney stayed in town at the Lee hotel and picked Debbie up from school each day. They had planned a June wedding. Hank and Cary went back to the cabin and lived, as the mansion had been designed and was now under construction. Cole was used as the contractor. The place was immense. It had ten bedrooms and contained over eight thousand square feet. They had hired some of Eduardo's kin as servants, but were not treated as servants, but more like friends. The servants were paid well.

Eduardo was talking to Hank and Cary about his cousins that worked there. He said, "I'll bet you pay them too much," and everyone laughed."

After their marriage, Debbie and Barney moved into the mansion. There were numerous parties held there. Most of the people were from Verdi. Verdi now was large enough to afford a full time marshal, so Hank and Barney were relieved of that duty.

The new marshal was named, Roscoe Evers. He was a no nonsense person. He said very little, but had abrupt actions for those who perpetrated the law.

Two violent men, who were said to have killed a sheriff in Kansas, and one in Missouri, had come to town. Roscoe had heard about them. He was just leaving the saloon when they came into the saloon. He knew who they were from a flier that had been sent to him.

Roscoe was not one to start trouble. He thought if they just came in for a drink and moved on, none of Verdi's citizens would be in danger. He returned to his office and pulled up their flier again and studied it.

Arthur Amos came into his office about a half-hour later and said, "There are two hard cases that are drinking in the saloon. They were bragging about two sheriffs that they killed. They said they would probably kill our sheriff if he came into the saloon."

"Where are they located in the saloon, Amos?"

"Just as you come in, look straight ahead and they are at the table against the wall."

Roscoe picked up a double barreled shotgun and walked down to the saloon. Amos was following him. Before they entered Roscoe said,

"You go in first, Amos, and if they are still against that back table, put your hand on your head."

Amos complied and put his head on his head. Both men had their guns out and were making a man dance as they fired at his feet.

Roscoe walked in with the shotgun ready to shoot. As he came in, he fired the shotgun at both men. They were nearly cut in half. Roscoe didn't stop walking. He went straight to the bar, leaned his shotgun against the bar and said, "I'll have a rye, Sam."

Everyone was amazed at his calmness. He then said, "Send someone for the undertaker and clean up that mess."

Word then passed around to other communities about Verdi's marshal and outlaws rode clear of Verdi.

Chapter 12

THE MISSIONARIES AND TROUBLES

The missionary group who came to Ben, the chief and Doctor Samuels" church told them about their mission. The three were all members of an independent Bible church back East. The missionaries told them they were headed for a Sioux reservation near Cheyenne, and were in desperate need of help.

They explained that the Sioux had troubles with alcoholism and the people needed Christian guidance. There were three women and one man. None of them related. Two of the women were in their twenties, and one of the women was near forty. The man was just over fifty and a recent widower.

The man said, "We don't even know the language, and have no clue how to treat alcoholism. The four of us prayed, and told God that we were available and would go, but that we would need his intervention."

Ben looked at the chief and he said, "We know a little about that, as I can cure men of alcoholism. I also speaks the language."

They all looked at the chief and he said, "If Ben comes with me, I'll go with you."

One of the women immediately said, "Let's pray and thank God for his mercy."

She said, "Lord, we know You led us here to these men. We have followed your leading and have no skill, but we are available to you. We saw no way of helping, but came as you had laid this problem on our hearts. When we received the letter from a Christian man at the reservation calling for help, we answered your call. Thank you for providing the men for this job. In Christ's name we pray this." The women were all crying and the three were in awe of their dedication to God.

Ben said, "We will need a few weeks to put our businesses in order. We run several businesses, but we believe that a partner of ours can take up the slack by engaging more employees. He's a Christian himself, and will see that we need to go."

After meeting the missionaries, Winston and the board took the responsibility of helping replace them. All understood their calling and Winston said, "If you will help us engage some people before you go, I think we can manage. It is nearing Christmas and you both need to be here for Hank's and Cary's wedding."

Ben said, "Yes, I love them and know they want us here."

The missionaries stayed at the Lee hotel and even joined in the work of cleaning and cooking. They could all see that the Lee family were Christians.

The wedding was held. Cary held on to Ben a long time and said, "I will always love you, Ben. You are very dear to me."

Two weeks later, they were off to Cheyenne. As they were traveling in a stagecoach Ben asked, "How did you get together, you seem to be unattached.

The man, named Bob Hanigan, said, "My wife died a month before we received the letter asking our church to provide help. As I am fixed financially, I decided to dedicate my life to Christian service. Ellen and Marsha lost their husband's in the war and were already in the missionary service. We all read the letter several time. Ellen was the first to say, 'I'm going.' Marsha said, 'If you're going, I'm going.' That convinced me to go with them, as it is still a man's world. Daphne was also in the Lord's service and asked to come with us.

"As we discussed the mission, we all knew we had no experience and were only available. We took the train to Denver, and were led to your church. God did the rest."

Ben said, "God works in mysterious ways. I would have never guessed I would be a missionary. But both the chief and I have experience treating alcoholism. The chief and I were brought together in a miraculous manner also, so you see all of this is in God's hands."

One of the younger women, named Marsha took Ben's hand and squeezed it. Ben looked at her and her eyes met his. Ben thought her face was that of an angel.

They arrived at the reservation and had no place to stay. However, there were some empty tents as some of the tribe had left. The chief and Ben took one tepee with the male missionary and the three women took another. Wood for fuel was nonexistent as the tribe had used up all the wood around the reservation."

The Indian agent was in Cheyenne. Ben said, "We can't live in tepees. If we are to stay anytime, we must have a building to live in. There must also be someplace to meet the people of the tribe needing medical attention."

The next day they looked at the Indian agents building. It was very large and was used to dole out supplies. It had a meeting room and quarters for the Indian agent.

Ben said, "The chief and I will go to town and find the Indian agent and persuade him to let us renovate his building, so we can do the work we need to do.

All agreed and Ben and the chief left the group and went to town. They found the Indian Agent, Bill Brown, and he said, "I have no money for such an operation, but if you have the resources, you have my permission."

114

Ben found a contractor and told him what he wanted to do. The contractor, Mike Rogers, said, "I will have to see the building first, then I can give you a price. It had been over four hours since they left as they stopped for lunch.

When they returned they were horrified. The male missionary, Bob Hanigan, was lying on the ground and had been scalped. Every tepee had been burned and no one was there.

Ben quickly examined Hanigan. He was dead.

They found an Indian woman who had hidden during the raid. She said, "They took your women and all the tribe. They had many horses. I don't know where they went, as I found a place to hide and stayed there until they left."

Ben said, "We'll find them."

The chief said, "We need to consult with the Army. We need to go after them, but we don't know where to go. Besides, we would do no good just the two of us."

Ben said, "That makes sense. Where is Army headquarters?"

The contractor gave him the directions and the chief and Ben left.

***

The commanding officer, Colonel Clemens, said, "I'll gather a troop and go after them. Please come with us. Being you know the women, you will be of help. They left about two hours later. Ben and the Chief had been furnished army horses. The troop included several wagons and two light cannons. Before he left, Colonel Clemens had his executive officer prepare another troop of equal size, to follow them as soon as it could be organized. The executive officer had wired another fort to send five hundred troops. Controlling the Sioux was a great priority with the army. They wanted to overwhelm the Indians and bring them back to reservations or exterminate them.

They found the tracks the Indians had left and followed them. They had Indian scouts who were ahead of the column. The scouts reported back that the Indians were camped in a stronghold some five miles ahead. The scout said that the Sioux knew they were being pursued, and were waiting for the attack.

Clemens decided to approach the Indian encampment, but not attack. He wanted to surround the encampment and bombard the stronghold after his executive officer arrived with several more cannons.

When Ben heard this news he went to Clemens and said, "There are three women missionaries with the Indians. If you bombard the camp, they may be killed."

Colonel Clemens said, "You have to look at the big picture, Mr. Lee. If we try to attack their position, many of my troop will be killed. By staying at a distance and just using our cannons, we can bring them into submission without killing a lot of troopers. It is a matter of your three missionaries against many of my troopers. Do you understand that?"

Ben hung his head and said, "Yes. I guess you have thought this out. Do you think I could go into their camp and try to bargain with them?"

"I think the only thing you would accomplish is to die a terrible death. Most of these Indians are desperate. They're young, and can see that they will probably die anyway, so they want to die a warrior's death. They don't think like we do. Reasoning with them is useless. Most of them think that all white people are their enemy, and we are to a certain extent. We have taken their land and killed their people. I understand their thinking, but I am charged with protecting the citizens of America, and I will carry out my duty as best I can."

Ben left and went back to where the chief had made them a camp. It was away from the soldiers. Ben said, "Do you think we could go into that Indian camp and get the women?"

"No, you couldn't, but maybe I could. I can tell them I am a medicine man and the Great Spirit has sent me to council with them. I more than likely will be killed, but I can at least try. I just wish I had some Indian clothing."

"Maybe you could buy some from the scouts."

The chief agreed and they went to one of the scouts. Ben gave him a five dollar gold piece for his clothes. The scout thought they were nuts, and quickly changed clothes with the chief.

The chief now looked like an Indian except for his hair. He looked at Ben and said, "If we never see each other again, know that you are my brother and my best friend. Ben wept and hugged him. He then said, "Go with God."

The chief slipped out of camp and past the sentries. It was about dusk as he made his way toward the Indian encampment. Two Indians were on guard and the chief spoke to them in Sioux. He said, "I am Lesta Katonka, a medicine man. I have come to council with the leaders of your tribe. I was sent here by the Great Spirit."

They took him to a fire where many of the elders sat. One of the elders knew the chief. He had known him years ago when they raided together. The elder was Wisingo. He stood and said, "I know this warrior. We made war on the white man in the old days. He was a great horse thief."

Katonka said, "I am now being used by the Great Spirit to bring you wisdom. If you stay here, the white soldiers are going to use the guns with the great voice on you. They will not attack, but stay where they are and rain the large balls into your camp. They will continue this until your people are no more."

No one said anything for awhile and the chief knew they were each letting his speech steep within them. After what was about three to four minutes Wasingo said, "What happened to your hair, Katonka?"

The white man took me and cut it off. They thought by doing this, you would not hear me. They also put me in white man's clothes, but I traded with one of their scouts, his clothes for mine. He thought it a good trade, but didn't realize that the white man had put these clothes on me for a purpose. I have told you what will happen, you must now decide what you must do."

One of the leaders spoke and said, "You are very brave to come to us. We know the white soldiers may kill you for this. Do you want to stay with us?"

"Katonka thinks if I were to go to them and tell them that you will give up the White women, they may leave. It may just be a foolish try, but they may trade. The white eyes put great pride in their women. We are not that foolish, but they are. What have you got to lose, only three white women, who are worth nothing. They have not been taught to work, and would bear you weak children."

The council thought of this awhile. There was some argument. It took about fifteen minutes then the chief stood and said, "Your words are wise, Lesta Katonka. You are brave. We will allow you to take the white women. As you say, they are worthless. Will you go to the pony soldiers and ask them for a trade? Tell them we will send the white women with you when you return in exchange for them leaving and returning to their fort."

It was settled and the chief made his way back. It was easy to slip past the sentries, and he was soon back to where Ben was. He told Ben what had happened, and they went to Colonel Clemens. The chief then told what he had done.

Clemens said, "I didn't even know you were an Indian. You took great risk in what you did. I will have to think about this some. We can save the women, but we must return to the fort. I can do that, but once I reach the fort, I will have to prepare for an engagement against them. I will tell my superiors what happened, and let them decide. They will know I had the opportunity to maybe end this war, but at the expense of losing three women missionaries. This could end my career, but if it saves three women, so be it."

Ben said, "You are a brave man Colonel Clemens and a hero in my books."

"Thank you, Ben."

The chief was sent back and told the Indian council. The chief said, "The colonel will turn his troops toward home tomorrow morning. I am to follow with the women a few miles back. You will be allowed to send braves with us in case the white men go back on their word. Your braves can then kill all of us if that happens."

The chief said, "You will always be welcome at our fire, Katonka. The Great Spirit has touched you."

The next day the troops returned to their fort. Ben was told what the chief had done and that he would be coming soon. The chief followed with the women and five braves. After ten miles or so, the braves each saluted the chief and left. Ben had held back and met them soon after the braves departed. When the braves left the older woman, Daphne put her arms around the chief and said, "I love you, Doctor Lee. You put your life on the line for us. Each woman then hugged the chief.

Daphne stayed right with the chief and he liked that. He could tell she really did love him. Ellen said, "I want to go home. This has changed me. I can no longer stay her. I think God will have another mission for me. She had no money, but Ben bought her ticket and gave her twenty dollars to eat on. She went back to Virginia where her folks lived.

They reached the Indian agents quarters. Bill Brown was there packing. He said, "I've been recalled, as the Indians are all gone. Marsha asked Ben what he was going to do.

Ben said, "Doctor Lee and I have decided that we will always be together where ever that may be. We have lived in Denver for the past six years and have a thriving business there. Doctor Lee has a medical clinic there with another doctor who is also included in our business. I'll start from the beginning tonight, so Daphene can hear it, too. I think she is sweet on Doctor Lee."

"I don't think she is sweet on him, I think she's in love with him," Marsha said. "You say he is part Indian?"

"No, not part, he is an Indian. I'll explain our relationship tonight at dinner. I want to celebrate. I want to buy you girls new clothes and a hot bath in the best hotel in Cheyenne. When we are all dressed up, we will have a splendid dinner.

"You must be rich, Ben."

"No, but I came into a lot of money when I was fourteen. I'll explain that also tonight."

When they reached Cheyenne, they went to a fine hotel and rented rooms for the two girls and the chief and Ben. They then went shopping. Ben bought each of the girls three dress, underwear, stockings, shoes and hats. They were overwhelmed, but accepted the gift graciously. They went back to the hotel so the girls could bathe. Ben and the chief went shopping. Ben insisted that they buy a suit, new boots, under garments, new shirts and hats.

They then went to a barbershop and had a bath, a shave and a haircut. At the hotel Ben insisted they wear their new suits, new boots and hats. They now looked splendid.

They picked up the girls at seven and were amazed how beautiful they looked. Daphne had been a hairdresser and their hair looked marvelous. Their new gowns fit them perfectly and the men were amazed at the transformation.

They went to the hotel dining room and were placed at a table near the front window. After they ordered Ben told their tale of him losing his family and the chief being thrown out his tribe. Ben said, "We then formed a new tribe, called the *Ghost Tribe*." He laughed then and said, "It is now a corporation." He told of how each person joined their tribe and how it grew and was still growing."

Daphne said, "Do you think we could be part of all that?"

"You already are," Ben said. I'm sure Doctor Lee wouldn't let you go, you fit together."

Daphne leaned toward the chief and he put his arm around her and said, "You'll be with me, so you will fit."

Marsha said, "I want to be where you are Ben. Am I being too forward?"

"No, I like candidness. I'll have to tell you about Cary Elder when we first met, but I will wait until we are alone to tell you."

After the meal, the chief and Daphne went for a walk. Ben and Marsha went another direction. Ben and Marsha were in a park where a bench was available for them to sit on. He then told Marsha about rescuing Cary and how they bathed together nude and thought nothing of it.

Marsha said, "Do you love her?"

"Yes, but like a sister, now. She married Hank Dobbs last Christmas." We once thought we would marry, but Cary's love was mostly gratitude and my love was from lonesomeness. When we were surrounded by other people, we realized we were more brother and sister than lovers. That gave Hank time to be with her, and they fell in love."

"I don't know how she let a man like you go, Ben."

"You may feel the same after you are surrounded by loving people, and life becomes good again. You've been through a trying time, and it will take some time for you to think normally."

"Maybe, we will just have to let life play out. Right now, I want to be with you alone, with your arms about me. I feel safe and warm. I was freighted so deeply I just knew my life was over.

"I think Daphne is in love with Dr. Lee. He's the strong silent type. Daphne looks beyond him being an Indian. She may get Doctor Lee to marry her. I think he misses a wife. She may be very good for him."

"Yes, I think so, too. He's a wonderful man."

"He's the closes friend I ever had. We felt the bond almost immediately. He had lost his tribe, and I had lost my family. We just had each other until we got Cary. She was the same way. She had lost everything and needed us badly. I remember the look in her eyes when we were sitting on that porch. She was filthy, and had sores all over her.

She looked at me and asked if I were an angel. It nearly made me cry, as I saw the absolute despair she felt. Love poured over me for her. I wanted to help her so badly. I can still see her standing in that stream stark naked just talking to me like I was just another girl. She felt no shame, and I didn't either, only love. I think that's when life is the happiest for me. When I see someone hurting like Doctor Samuels. He was desperate, also. I was sitting up front driving a buggy. The doctor needed a drink so badly that I could nearly feel it myself. Alta crawled over into the backseat with him and took him in her arms like he was her baby. They cried together as the doctor needed love more than a drink. As they cried, I cried. It was one of the most poignant moments of my life just to witness the love that passed between them."

"You are a very deep person, Ben. I hope we fall in love. I loved my first husband. We were both young and crazy in love. There was probably more lust than love. However, he was taken from me. I could hardly bear it, but I filled that void with Jesus. I have often wanted to love Jesus much more than Harold. I want to be desperately in love with Jesus. We have never seen him, but I know he is real. I see a lot of Jesus in you, Ben. You and Doctor Lee love Jesus so much it shows in you."

"Yes, when he chose to go and try to bargain with the Indians, he just took it as something he had to do, like watering the horses or something like that. If fear was in him, I couldn't see it. He is a magnificent man and I thank God every night for bringing us together. Together we are much better than apart."

"It's sort of like a marriage, you two. You compliment each other."

"I hope now Daphne can give him the love he lost with his first wife. He deserves that kind of love. Maybe it is God's reward to him for living his life like Jesus."

They returned to the hotel and Marsha was given a room once occupied by Cary. Cary had left many nice things. When Sarah was showing the room to her said, "Use anything here. I know Cary would want you to. She is a very nice person and I hope you can meet her soon."

Marsha said, "Ben told me about her. He told it in such a way that I could just see the love that passed between them. I'm amazed that God didn't bring them together."

"I observed the two and really thought they would marry. Cary wanted Ben to sleep with her, but Ben is strong in his beliefs, and knew it was not right. Had they slept together it would have turned out differently. I think as they were around all of us they saw each other more as brother and sister. They still love each other deeply. Cary would give her life for him, but the lust left them some how. Hank is much more suited to Cary than Ben. They really have a thing for each other.

"When I met Robert I thought him the most handsome man in the world. He was so caring. Mother encouraged me, as she saw the same thing I did. It took me awhile, but I finally got him to love me. He was reluctant at first, because of the loss of his arm. But once he saw it didn't matter to me, he loved me like I always wanted a man to love me."

"My with all this love around me, I think I will be very happy here."

Chapter 13 ═══════════════════════

BACK IN DENVER

Being in Denver with the Lee family worked out well for the two missionaries. They integrated into the work force easily. Daphne, became a nurse and receptionist at the medical building and Marsha worked into the bookkeeping department as Sarah really needed the help with Alta gone.

Marsha was a smart woman and learned the bookkeeping easily. Winston wanted Ben to be an over-all manager. He wanted him to oversee all the different businesses, and fix problems before they grew. He was good at this as his personality was outgoing, and he always wore a smile. He also handled the needs in the labor force. He interviewed and hired people. He also handled the discipline. He did it in such a manner that the people being disciplined were never mad at him. He just described the problem and told them if they would followed a plan he had for them then everyone would be happy. When they followed his plan they worked out well. When they didn't and Ben fired them they always said, 'I fired myself and left liking Ben.

Winston said, "Ben, to me you are this companies best employee. You can't begin to know how you help me in particularly. I know more about what's going on than I ever did. It keeps us out of trouble. Even Martin says you are the most valuable person in our organization. I remember you telling me that you feel useless just going from business to business learning what is going on, but I can assure you, our business is much stronger because of you. You save us ten times the amount you're paid."

The corporation paid each member of the their trust a monthly salary. It was enough that all had more than they needed. If something came up that one of the members needed extra money, all he had to do is submit it to the board and it was granted.

Marsha and Ben still saw each other on a regular basis. Doctor Lee and Daphne, however, married. Ben felt some pressure as he knew Marsha loved him, but he was not quite ready. He decided to go back and reclaim the rest of his money that was hidden in the large iron box.

Ben told the chief he needed to pick up the remainder of his money. He said, "Now that the army is back, it will be safe. I want to drop by and see how Homer and Alta are doing."

The chief agreed that it would be safe. Ben talked to Winston about it. He said, "I hid about twenty to thirty thousand dollars that I need to recover. It used to be dangerous, but with the army having occupied the fort again, no Indians are anywhere near there."

Winston agreed that he should go pick up his money and said, "I'll cover for you, Ben."

One of the reasons Ben wanted to leave was that Marsha wanted him so much. She was at the point in her life where she wanted to be married. He thought she was more in love with marriage than she was with him. He loved her, but was not "in love," with her. He thought that maybe things would cool off with her if he were gone a few weeks.

He decided to drive a buggy because he wanted to bring back the iron box. He arrived at the way station and Homer and Alta were glad to see him. They introduced the new couple that Homer had hired. He wanted to increase his crops and cattle holdings now that the Indians were gone. The stages were running again and the telegraph was now installed from Kansas City to Denver.

As he was traveling toward the place where he had lost his family, he thought of all the changes that had been made. He was now twenty-one years old and could vote. However, he wasn't very political, as he had been so busy helping their company that he didn't even know who was running for office. He thought he would be more cognizant of that world when he returned.

He then thought of Marsha. He knew she would be a good wife, but he wasn't ready for a family. He compared her to Cary, but they were worlds apart. When he thought of Cary, the picture of her standing nude in that stream always came to mind. She too had changed. He liked the little girl that was so candid that it embarrassed him. He nearly laughed aloud when he thought of her standing there talking, not thinking anything about being nude before him. Although she had been passed around from one man to the other, he always thought of her as pristine. She loved him completely at that time. She wanted to sleep with him and he her, but he had better sense and over came his urges. Now she was married to Hank.

Hank seemed so mature and sure of himself. Barney, too. They were both ready for marriage, but he surely wasn't. He liked his freedom. He could come and go anywhere in the world, but with a wife he was bound to her. He thought, *"If I loved her so much I didn't want to go anywhere, then I would marry. But right now, I have the urge to travel."* He thought he might go back East, and maybe to England and France. The only thing stopping him was Marsha."

He had not made the advances, it was her. He kissed her some, but that also was her wanting to be kissed. He was not in love with her, but she was in love with him. He felt obligated, but why? It was just that he didn't want to hurt her feelings. He decided to write and tell her he needed to be away for awhile to think things out. She would understand that, and put two and two together, that he didn't want to be married.

He reached the place where his iron box was and had a hard time loading it onto his buggy. He had brought a light buggy, and it's seat laid down so he could sleep off the ground. He also could button it up to keep the mosquitoes out.

He traveled east after he finally got the iron box aboard. He decided that when he reached Kansas City, he would deposit his money and put the watches and rings in a safety deposit box. He did keep five thousand dollars. He wanted to live well.

At Kansas City he wrote Marsha a letter, telling her that he needed some time to himself to think things out. She took it the way he had intended. She thought, *"He is not in love with me and probably never will be. He would never come right out and say it, because he's too nice a person."*

He also wrote Winston and the others, telling them that he needed to be away for awhile. Winston knew immediately it was because of Marsha. He could see that she was in love with Ben, but he wasn't in love with her. Nothing was said, but most of them figured this out.

Lastly he wrote Homer and Alta and told them he was in Kansas City and had decided to go to New York City. This puzzled them. Alta then said, "He's running from a woman," and they both laughed.

She said, "I would have sworn that he and Cary would marry. They seemed so right for one another and Cary was so devoted to him."

Homer said, "Feelings change sometimes. I know Hank really loves her. They seem more suited than Ben and her. Cary changed once her folks came back into her life."

Ben was on the train to Chicago. He remembered the trip with his sisters. He wondered how they would have looked had they lived. He could not remember their faces and it grieved him. The only image he had was the bullet holes in their heads and their hair removed by the Indians. He decided to think of something else, but his mind moved back to his dad. He was such a good dad. Ben hoped that he would be as good, if he found someone to love.

He thought of Cary and how they seemed to drift apart once she left with her dad. What a tragedy. When she returned after her father and his partner were killed, she was a different person. He wondered how someone could change so radically. She was not that little girl who looked at him with those eyes that seemed to radiate love. She was harder somehow, like she had been through a war.

Ben remembered the men who returned from the war, and how they had changed. They were hard men who seemed to not let people into their lives. He had heard two women talk of their husbands, and how the war had changed them. He wondered if Cary had seen some terrible things that had changed her. Well, no use to go over that again, she had married Hank. They seemed to be meant for one another. He smiled to himself and thought, *"She grew up. Maybe I'm still a boy."*

After thinking of Cary, he felt alone. Marsha surely wasn't the answer. If she had not wanted him so badly, he may have wanted her, but she was so needy. He then tried to think of New York City and what it would bring. He knew no one there. Could he make friends?"

Ben left the train at Grand Central Station. It was the busiest place he had ever seen. He sat down and just watched the people. Everyone was in a hurry. Where were they all going?

He was on the sidewalk outside and saw a man with a tin cup. He didn't ask people to give to him, he just sat on a concrete slab and put out his cup. Every so often someone would put something in his cup.

Ben walked up and noticed he had but one arm. He said, "Have you lived in the city long?"

"All my life except for the war. As you can see, I lost my arm there. However, I'm not grieving about that. Many of my close friends lost their lives."

"How would you like to be employed by me. I will pay you a dollar a day and feed you."

"What would be my duties?"

"To show me the city. I want to know all about it. Do you have a family?"

"Not anymore. I couldn't make a living, so my wife left me and married a whole man. I don't blame her and told her so. We left friends. No one will hire me, and I have little education, so I have to beg for my living."

"Where do you live?"

"Here on the street, where ever I can curl up without the cops rousting me. I've been put in jail several times, but now most of the policemen know me, and leave me alone. Most of them were in the war, too."

"What's your name?"

"Thomas Jefferson Adams. My mother wanted me to be the president, I suppose. You can call me Jeff as my father was known as Tom. Their both gone now. I'm glad they can't see me now. I would shame them."

"Well, you won't have to think about that for awhile. The first thing we're going to do is get you a bath, a haircut, a shave then buy you new clothes. We will just put those in the garbage. Let's go."

They went to a nice store for men. Ben was astounded at the prices, but he thought, "*What better way to give to the Lord?*"

They then went to a nice hotel and rented a room with two beds and a bathroom. Jeff bathed and put on the new clothes. They then went to a barbershop and both had a shave and a haircut. As they were in the chairs, Ben said, "I just thought of something. Maybe we could start a business giving tours to people who are visiting the city. Do you know if anyone has that kind of business?"

"No, but it sounds like something I could do. How would people know about our business?"

"We can go to the hotels and put up a poster in each hotel telling them about our service. We could also tell the hacks about our service, and tell them we will give them a fee for every person who they send our way. We will need a carriage and you can be dressed nicely, and sit with the tourist. I'll drive where you tell me to go. I will also wear a costume."

"That would cost a lot of money."

"There is always an investment in nearly every enterprise. Here, we would just have the expense of the carriage, horse, costumes and posters."

"You are a smart one. Do you own a business?"

"Several businesses in Denver, Colorado. One of them is a taxi service, so I know all about business and what it takes to succeed. First you must provide a service that is needed, and then charge a reasonable price. It's as simple as that."

They spent the rest of the day going to four major hotels and telling about their service. Ben said, "It may enhance your business by providing your guest with an added attraction."

All the hotel liked the idea. They had posters made and bought an expensive buggy that they had painted a bright red in oppose to the yellow taxis. On the side of the buggy it read "tours." It was large enough to seat six people. Ben made the seat by him to swivel so it could turn around toward the riders. If six people were there, Jeff could sit by him.

Jeff mapped out what he thought was a good tour that took just a half day. They would leave at nine in the morning and return by noon. They would then leave at one in the afternoon with another tour that would last until four. Business went well from the start.

They began making lots of money, as they charged what the Broadway shows charged. Most people thought it well worth the price. Ben began to know most of the hotel staff and was quite popular with them as was Jeff. After two months Ben found a driver to take his place. He had taught Jeff how to handle the money and to log every person, and their fee into a ledger. They had a bank account and Ben made Jeff do all the business with them. Ben found a lawyer who drew up formal papers for their company with Jeff as the president.

Ben said, "I've got you started, Jeff. I will have you place twenty percent of the net receipts into my private account." He had already recouped his investment money. "I'm leaving for Miami, Florida next week."

Jeff thanked him profusely and Ben left on the train the next Monday.

Chapter 14

MIAMI FLORIDA

Ben made several acquaintances on the train and had a nice time with his travel. He stopped in Savanna, Georgia and stayed there two days. He met an elder couple at a restaurant inadvertently. The man was eating a steak and got it caught in his throat. Ben knew the man was in deep trouble and grabbed the man up from the floor by his waist. This caused the man to bend at the waist, forcing the air from his lungs which dislodged the meat stuck in his throat. He was nearly blue when he gasped for air.

A doctor was there and turned to Ben and said, "You saved this man's life. Another minute and he would have been dead. The wife of the man then fainted as she realized how close to death her husband was.

The next morning, Ben received an invitation to attend a party at the house of the man he had saved. Ben just thought it was a small gathering to formally thank him, so he attended. To his amazement, the people lived in a mansion and when he entered, many people were there and they all clapped as he entered. The mayor of Savanna was there and presented Ben with the Key to the city. The doctor who was there told how Ben could see the man was in dire straits, and went into action. He said, "Had not Mr. Lee not taken the action that he did, our favorite son, Lon Mason, would be in the cemetery now.

We would have all lost a treasure to this city."

Lon's wife, Lara, was now crying as several of the women were. Ben thought, "This guy must be really loved. Everyone shook Ben's hand and many women hugged him. One woman actually kissed him. She explained that she was Lon's sister and how grateful she was."

Lon said, "Our daughter, Amy, lives in Miami and Lara has already written her. She will be at the train station to meet you. She will have you stay at her home, which is right on the water. We have been there several times and a finer place does not exist. It's not as large as our home, but it is much more suitable to live. The guestroom has large windows that open onto a balcony with a great view.

Ben said, "Thank you all for this party. I feel so inadequate. I don't feel like the hero you make me out to be. I'm just a simple man from Denver, Colorado. As a matter of fact, I'm in a tribe we call the *Ghost Tribe*. I lost my family in a battle with the Indians when coming west and I continued on foot. During my travel I came upon an Indian sitting alone. He had been kicked out of his tribe because of his age. He had been educated by missionaries and was quite educated.

"We decided to form our own tribe with displaced people like ourselves. We added people as we went. Our tribe grew with extraordinary people. When we reached Denver we started several businesses, and have done quite well. I decided to take some time off and see some of America. I toured New York and decided to see the South. I'm amazed how beautiful Savanna is, but its people are more splendid. I will cherish this party the rest of my life. Finer people cannot be found." Everyone clapped.

Just like Lon said, a women with beautiful blond hair was waiting for him. Lon had said, "When you get off the train, look for a beautiful blond woman. She will be the most gorgeous woman you have ever seen, so you will have little trouble finding her."

Ben walked toward her. A broad smile crossed her face. She said, "Mother said you were young and good looking. You are all of that. I want to first thank you for saving my father's life," and with that she hugged him and kissed him on both cheeks. They went to a buggy driven by a man in a uniform.

Ben said, "Hello, I'm Ben Lee. The man was surprised that Ben addressed him and took Ben's hand that was thrust out."

Amy said, "You are a very polite man. I have never seen anyone acknowledge Porter. He's a valued employee and a family treasure. He was my daddy's valet for years. I've known him all my life, so when I moved to Miami, daddy wouldn't let me go without Porter. I feel much safer with him around.

"Mother wrote several pages about you. It was actually the longest letter she ever wrote me. You really impressed my folks and rightfully so, as you saved daddy's life."

Ben said, "I thank you for your hospitality." Ben had noticed the large diamond wedding rings she wore and said, "Is your husband at work?"

"No, he passed away a year ago, or he would have been right with me to meet you as he loved daddy. I think he loved daddy more than he did his own father as the two were together all the time until he took a job in Miami."

"What business was he in?"

"He and a friend of his had an investment business. Last year he was found on the beach. He had been shot. To my knowledge he had no enemies. His partner said that everyone that they did business with, were extremely happy with them.

"His wallet was stolen and the police thought he had just been robbed and killed. That didn't seem right to me. Roger was very careful and had a derringer hidden under his coat. It was still there when they found him. If he were robbed, I think the robbers would have searched him and found the derringer. They also didn't take his watch or ring. Both were gold and worth quite a lot. I could do nothing about it.

"His partner, Lloyd Summers, offered to buy my interest out, but I told him I wanted to wait a year and see where I was then. He could tell I wouldn't waver, so he left it at that. I get a monthly income, but it's not nearly what Roger made when working. Daddy gave me a legacy, which is quite substantial, so I have no financial worries. However, Roger's murder still sticks in my craw."

Ben said, "If I can be of any assistance, please call on me. I'm a businessman and understand much about the investment business. Our company has invested in the market quite heavily."

"We won't talk of these things for awhile. I want to introduce you to Miami and its society. There's a party next Saturday. I would like to show you off. You are some younger than me, so people's tongues won't wag too much, I hope."

Ben's room was better than it was described. He loved the balcony. He had unpacked and bathed. He was about to go downstairs when he heard a knock on his door. He answered it. It was Amy with two glasses in her hands. They were mint juleps.

Amy said, "Everyone should be treated with a mint julep when they arrive in the South. Let's sit out on the balcony, sip these, and get to know each other. I would like to know all about you."

They sat and Ben told her as candidly as he could his life story. She was very impressed."

She said, "Tell me about Cary. You kind of glazed over her. I feel you were close to her."

Ben decided to tell the whole truth about them in great detail. At the end she said, "People do change. I feel you both missed a deep love. Something happened to her while she was gone with her father. You said her father was killed. I bet she witnessed his killing and took revenge. That alone will change someone. What did she say about Odom?"

"She just said he left."

"Yes, but she didn't say where he went. And all his hands just rode away. Why?

"I bet she did them in. I don't know why, but I feel she did them in. That is what changed her. You said she became hard. I can see that making one hard. I know you will never ask her, but I think she would tell you she couldn't live with what she did and you. You are too pure. You tell how pure the chief is, but you are just like him."

"I guess we are alike. I know we think much alike."

"Now Marsha, she's a different story. You're running from her. Am I right?"

"I guess you are. You seem to know as much about me as I do myself. How do you do that?"

"I have taken an interest in you. Very few people have interested me. As a matter of fact, only Roger brought out that interest before you. He said, the same thing as you said, 'that I knew as much about him as he did.'"

"You are someone I like to be around. I want you to help me solve Rodger's murder. If you're willing, I would like to take you to Roger's office and have you take his place. I will tell Lloyd that you will be his new partner. What do you say?"

"I would like to go to work for you. It will also give me an opportunity to invest some of my assets without having to pay a brokerage fee."

"They had dinner that night on her balcony. They had rooms that adjoined the same balcony. The large windows acted as doors. They had dressed and Ben wore a white dinner jacket with a white shirt and a black bowtie. His pants were black, and he looked his best.

Amy wore an orange gown that accentuated her blond hair that was past her shoulders. She wore a diamond necklace.

Ben had never seen a more lovely woman in his life. She thought the same. Her first husband was a fine looking man, but Ben was his equal. They eyed each other for awhile and then Amy said, "We are both interested, I see."

Ben smiled and said, "Any man on earth would be interested. You are past beautiful, you're gorgeous."

Amy said, I'm twenty-seven, Ben. You are some younger than me, but you're more mature than men in their thirties or forties. You have a demeanor about you that makes a woman feel comfortable and secure."

"Do I feel a romance coming on?" Ben asked.

"Maybe, but we need to be around each other longer."

"Yes, I think you're right. Love needs to grow like a plant. You need to water it and care for it and watch it grow.

"Tell me more about Roger's business partner."

"Lloyd is outgoing and has a nice personality. He is smart and ambitious."

"Explain the ambition of Lloyd."

"He always wanted to move too fast from Roger's point of view. Roger never liked to take risks and this irked Lloyd.

"I wonder how he will react to me. When you tell him I am to take Roger's place?"

"What can he do but accept you. I own as much of the business as he does."

The next day at the office, Amy introduced Ben as a trusted friend. She then said, "I want him to take Roger's place. He is a smart business man. My parents adore him. He once saved daddy's life. Mother wrote pages about him."

Lloyd said, "You have astounded me, Amy. I don't know what to say. Maybe we should go slower on this?"

"No, I want Ben to integrate into the business right away. He's very astute and will represent me like Roger did."

"Well, I see you've made up your mind. I'll show you your office, Ben, then later brief you on where we are. As I have way too many clients, I'll turn some of them over to you as quickly as possible."

Ben quickly became functional. He studied stocks avidly, and gave good advice to his clients. His personality was his best asset. Everyone saw him as an expert, which he wasn't, but appeared to be. Lloyd was amazed at his ability. They began to make more money as Ben brought enthusiasm to the business. He had some great ideas. He put an ad in the paper everyday. He had a billboard put up advertising their brokerage firm. Little by little Ben began to learn the financial end of their business. He went over the books with a fine toothed comb.

By the fourth month, he could see how Lloyd was not reporting all of the income he generated. He decided to discuss this with Amy.

She got a look in her eye that Ben thought he recognized. He said, "You think he killed Roger don't you?"

"I'm beginning to. I would advise you to never tell Lloyd what you've found."

"He doesn't even know that I study the books. I have only done that after hours. Do you still have that derringer and its scabbard that Roger wore?"

"Yes, I think you should start wearing it."

"They were leaving for their rooms and Ben followed her into her room to get the derringer. She handed it to him and said, "Why haven't, you tried to kiss me, Ben?"

"You said, we needed to know each other more."

"I meant that we shouldn't go overboard. I need to be hugged once in awhile. A kiss would be nice, too."

After Ben strapped on the derringer to see how it fit, Amy came into his arms and kissed him. He was startled, but liked it. They became closer, and soon their bodies touched when they kissed."

They went to a lot of parties, so now everyone saw them as a couple. Tongues did wag, but they didn't care.

Ben began to photograph the books. It was obvious that Lloyd was skimming the books.

Ben had met a detective at a party and befriended him. His name was Larry Minor. He talked of embezzlement with Larry. After a couple of weeks they began to meet for drinks after work. Larry had started a detective agency after he retired from the police force, and had several men working for him.

After he and Ben were good friends, Ben said, "Larry, I think my partner is not reporting some of his end of the business."

Larry said, "That's called embezzlement, Ben."

"I would like to hire you to handle this. I have been studying the books for six months now, and have photographed key pages. Would you take the job?"

"Sure. How do you want to go about this?"

"I'm not sure. Amy thinks he killed Roger when he confronted him. She has no evidence, though. The police said it was a murder, caused by robbery. However, when he was found on the beach his wallet was gone, but not a derringer he was wearing, or his ring and watch. That didn't make sense if he were killed by a robber."

"Yes, I remember the case. They had no one to blame, so they just called it a robbery. I see where you're going and it looks like Amy may be right, if Lloyd is skimming. I will give you some advise, don't ever tell Lloyd you suspect him.

"If you will give me the key to your place, I'll have an expert in auditing books, go over them and make a report. If he finds that Lloyd is doing what you say he is, you will have to bring charges against him. He may beat the rap, and that would end your business."

"No, it would only end our relationship. I would open another business. I'm only doing this to expose him, and maybe find out if he killed Roger."

Ben decided not to tell Amy. It would just worry and upset her. He now loved her and didn't want her involved.

The next week as Ben was going to bed, Amy said, "I have the feeling that you're involved with something dangerous."

"What?"

"You have to tell me, Ben. I feel a tenseness about you that was not there a few weeks ago."

Ben then told her the whole thing. She said, "Keep me up to date, and keep that derringer handy. I nearly know Lloyd killed Roger."

Larry now was certain Lloyd was embezzling. He even thought it would hold up in court. When he was telling this to Ben, Ben said, "I have a plan. I will let you into my office, and you can be in the closet with your gun. I will bring Lloyd into my office and tell him I have hired a detective team to go over the books and they found he was embezzling. I will then see his reaction."

Larry agreed and they set it up for the next day. It went down just like they planned it. Lloyd came into his office and Ben told him.

Ben asked, "Is this why you killed Roger?"

Lloyd pulled out a gun and said, "Yes. Just like you, he threatened to expose me. I guess you're headed to the same beach where I left Roger."

At that time Larry said, "Don't move or you're a dead man."

Lloyd froze. He was stunned. Larry said, "Drop the gun or I'll plug you."

Lloyd dropped the gun, and Larry handcuffed him.

Lloyd said, "I knew you were smarter than Roger. Unlucky for me you were too smart."

At the hearing Lloyd copped a plea, and was given thirty years. He was made to turn over his share of the business to Amy."

The trial was now over and Lloyd in prison. They had a great dinner. They were now having a brandy on the balcony. They kissed goodnight and went to bed. Ben tossed and turned and couldn't go to sleep. He knew he loved Amy, but did he love her to the point that he wanted to be with her all the time.

When they were at breakfast, Amy said, "Do you want to get married?"

"Ben waited awhile and then said, "I couldn't go to sleep last night as I was turning that over in my mind. I love you, but I don't know if we are to that point yet.

"I wish I were, but there it is."

Amy said, "I feel about the same. I love you and want to be around you, but I feel you still have reservations. If we are to marry, I don't want any reservations."

LOVE DEVELOPS

Back in Denver, Martin needed more help. They assigned Marsha to help him. By typing his letters and documents, she began to know the law. Martin saw this and began letting her handle things that were simple. This grew as she learned more. They began discussing the difficult problems, and she learned more and more. They worked closely together. Being close all the time, they begin giving each other looks.

At night Marsha thought, *"Ben will come back, but I don't feel about him as I use to. Martin is so manly. I shouldn't think of such things, but I want him."*

A week later they were looking for a law book and turned into each other. Their bodies met and they both just stood there. Martin took her in his arms and they kissed. The more they kissed the more passion came upon them.

Marsha stood back and said, "What about Ben?"

Martin said, "What about him. He's been gone six months now and never writes anymore. If he loved you, he would have written. I think he left to get away from you. He knew you loved him, but he didn't want to marry you. I hate to be so blunt, but that's the way I see it.

"I love you, and I think you love me. I want to marry you. It seems we were meant for each other. I've never seen anyone pick up

142

the law like you have. I think you did that because you wanted to be near me. I surely want you near me. I want to marry you. What do you say?"

"I suppose you're right. If he loved me, he would have written. I don't have the feelings I used to have for him. I do have feelings for you. I was thinking last night if it were just my lust that made me attracted to you. I think that is a lot of it, but I do admire and love you. I think this is why I studied so avidly, as I wanted to prove myself worthy."

"My gosh, I'm an alcoholic and always will be. You don't have to prove a thing to me. It's I who has to prove myself worthy of you."

Marsha came into his arms again and said, "I love you, Martin. Let's go tell Winston and ask his advice." Martin thought this the right move.

Winston listened to Martin tell about the absence of Ben and only the one letter.

He said, "I like many of the others thought he was running away from you, Marsha. I'm glad you and Martin love one another. I hope you marry."

"I would write Ben if I knew where he was."

"Well, you have my blessings and I'm sure most of the others feel the same way."

Two weeks later Marsha and Martin were married. Everyone was amazed, but all thought it was better, because they all thought Ben had gone away to keep from marrying Marsha.

***

After Lloyd was in prison. Ben informed his clients that he would be gone for a couple of months. He arranged for another broker to use his office and service his clients. The new broker actually had a staff that aided him. He didn't have that many clients of his own and Ben had many. They struck a deal that would give Ben and Amy half the profits, and both were satisfied with that.

They took a train across country to Denver. It took three days. However they utilized the Pullman service and the trip wasn't that tiring.

They went right to the hotel where Martin had his office. When they walked in Marsha was just coming into the lobby from Marin's office. She was sporting her wedding rings.

She saw Ben and froze. She then said, "You're going to kill me, Ben. I married Martin. It was a thing of passion that neither of us could stop. I hope I didn't break your heart?"

"No, Marsha, I knew we would not be married. That is why I left. As beautiful as you are, I knew you would find the man of your dreams. I'm glad you found Martin."

Marsha then noticed the beautiful blond at his side. She stood out, she was the most beautiful woman Marsha had ever seen. Marsha said, "May I help you, Ma'am."

Ben said, "This is a friend of mine, Marsha. We met in Miami and have a business together."

Marsha said, "My goodness, you are gorgeous. Let me get Martin."

She was gone just a minute or so and Martin came out. He saw Ben and said, "I guess you're going to be mad at me, but I can explain. It came over both of us so suddenly we couldn't believe it."

He then saw Amy and said, "My lord, is this your friend, Ben?"

"Yes, I wanted to show her the West and particularly the people of the Lee corporation. I want to introduce Amy to everyone. She knows all your names and much about all of you. After we leave here, we will go out to Verdi and see Hank and Cary. Are they still living in that mining shack?"

"Well, it's more than just a shack. You will be amazed. I won't tell you about it, I want you to just experience it like we did."

They stayed three days and everyone was pleased with Amy. They then left of Verdi.

They stopped at the donut shop and met a lot of people as it was the town's gathering place. Mildred said, "I've heard a lot about you, Ben. Cary really loves you."

Amy thought, *"I hope it's a sisterly love. Ben has an effect on women. I see other women looking at him all the time."*

They spent the night in the hotel and drove out the next day to the LOBO ranch. At the gate, they could see the mansion that was being built on the hill. It was magnificent. They knew this was what Marsha was telling them about when she said, "You will just have to experience it."

Although the mansion was not finished a part of it was and they went to the door.

They were let in by a Mexican woman with a smile on her face. Cary came into the room and on seeing Ben ran to him and held the embrace for a long time with her eyes closed. They then stood and just looked at one another. Cary said, "I will always love you, Ben. I remember standing in that stream naked as a jaybird, and I had a love for you I had never felt. I will always love you. You saved my life."

She then turned and saw Amy for the first time. She said, "My lord, Ben who is this? She makes every woman around her look plain."

Ben laughed and said, "This is Amy. We are business partners. She is a lot like me. When she saw me she saw a little boy who had lost his way and took compassion on me like I did you."

Cary walked forward and said, "You have the most wonderful man in the world. We might have married at one time, but our love turned to be more spiritual than lustful. That love is above all love as it is holy, like Ben is. If I could love Jesus as much as he does, I would have done more in this life than I could ever dream. He shows people the love that Jesus has for us, just being around him. The chief once said he heard a saying that an Italian priest said. I believe his name was St. Francis. He said, We must all tell people about Jesus, even if we have to use words.' Every time I see Ben, I understand more fully what St. Francis meant."

Amy said, "I think Ben told me more about you than anyone. He holds a great love for you. I could feel it when you two hugged. It was something that anyone would feel if they saw you. I'm glad you love each other. It makes me love you both.

"Is your husband about?"

'No, he's down at the other ranch with Barney. Let's all go down there. He might take all day. I'll go get Debbie. Barney married my sister."

Ben said, "We can go in our carriage," and they left. It took about a half-hour to get there. Barney and Hank were on the porch drinking coffee with Eduardo.

When they drove up, Eduardo crossed himself and said, "Sweet mother of God, an angel just descended from heaven."

Amy laughed and said, "Just get to know me and you may change your opinion."

Ben introduced Amy and Barney said, "I'm with Eduardo, you are as pretty as an angel."

Cary said, "As pure as Ben is, God sent her for him and he deserves her."

Hank said, "She's right, Amy. I've known him for over six years and he does deserve an angel and I'm glad it's you."

Eduardo put his head in the door and said, "Maria, God just sent an angel from heaven come see."

With large eyes Maria came and said, "You're right, Eduardo, and she crossed herself."

Amy said, "Thank you Maria, but a saint, I'm not."

Maria was preparing lunch and she said, "Please stay and eat with us. I want to get to know you. I have never seen anyone as pretty as you are."

Juanita was a splendid cook and Barney said, "Eduardo, after you ate the first meal that Maria prepared, I bet you proposed."

Eduardo said, "Yes, she is the greatest cook, but she is a better lover."

Juanita blushed and said, "Eduardo, please."

They had a splendid afternoon and Hank said, "Let's have a party tonight to celebrate Ben and Amy's coming to see us."

It was just a matter of rounding up the musicians from Verdi. They had them pass the word that everyone was invited. Even Cole and Mildred came. He was in Green Valley on a project. Someone told him about the party, so he went home. Mildred had closed the café and was getting dressed.

She said, "After they announced that a party was being held at the mansion, I knew no customers would come to the café. Greta and I decided we would go, also. The other two girls are coming, too."

The party was wonderful. Cary danced with Ben the most. Hank was standing by Amy who was resting as everyone of the men wanted to dance with her. Hank said, "I ought to be jealous, but I love seeing them together. It is almost holy to me. I think I love Ben nearly as much as she does. He's something."

Amy said, "I thought I could never love anyone as much as my first husband, but he isn't even in it with Ben."

Hank said, "Have you two discussed marriage?"

"Yes, but we decided to wait awhile. I'm six years older than Ben, Ben is just twenty-one and I think he needs some time."

"Yes, Ben is very cautious. He weighs things carefully before he acts. When I first met him, he was only about fourteen, but had the wisdom of an adult. Even my dad said that."

"You and Barney talk like he's your brother."

"We consider him as close as that."

The next day they stayed until afternoon, but wanted to get to Verdi for a early start to Denver.

Cary clung to Ben before they left. She said, "Why don't you live here with us, Ben? We would love to have you."

"No, Amy's folks need her and I wouldn't separate them. Maybe after they pass on."

She again hugged Ben then they were off. As they were driving, Amy said, "When you were dancing with Cary, Hank came up and said, 'Just look at them. Those two really love one another. He said, 'You would think I would be jealous, but I'm not at all.' He said, 'I think I love Ben nearly as much as Cary does.'"

Ben said, "Thank you for telling me that, Amy. It gives me a warm feeling."

"It should. I was looking at Hanks face as he was telling me that, while looking at you, and I felt a warm feeling of love."

They were in Verdi for dinner and Mildred fixed them a tender steak. It was scrumptious. They left at first light and were in Denver by nightfall.

Marsha had fixed up a room for each and had some fruit in a bowl on the dresser. They stayed two more days, then took the train to Kansas City. From there they took a riverboat to New Orleans where they spent another night seeing a show. From there they took a ship to Miami.

They were both glad to be home. Ben went back to work. He was now overwhelmed with customers. He advertised in the New York Times for a stockbroker. He receiver twenty- seven resumes. He and Amy went over them and finally settled on one.

He was a man of forty-two. He told how he was successful, but could not take the cold anymore. They both laughed and Amy said, "We can't let the man freeze to death. His children are grown and he needs a change."

Herbert Forest and his wife, Milly, came a week later. He was nice looking although some overweight. His wife clung to him like he was going to runoff. He worked out well, and brought in customers.

After Ben got to know him better he mentioned the fact of his wife clinging to him. Herbert said, "Her folks died when she was but a teen. She felt so alone she could hardly stand it. We lived down the street and Mother took her in. I'm five years older and was away to college most of the time. However, when I came home on holidays, I could tell she felt so alone that she could hardly stand it. I began hugging her and she fell madly in love with me. When I left for college my senior year she said, I don't think I can stand it when you leave. It pulled my heart strings and I said, 'Then I'll marry you and take you along.' That was the greatest decision I ever made. I got like her, I didn't want to be away from her. I used her as my secretary. No one knew she was my wife as she called me, Mr. Forest."

"Well, let's bring her into the office. We could use her." She was there everyday and always called Herbert, Mr. Forest.

***

Back in Denver, Dr. Samuels and a new doctor and Dr Lee had a thriving business. Daphne was the receptionist and wore a fresh white uniform each day. She made sure that her husband looked very professional. He wore his hair very short and was cleanly shaven and smelled good.

They were very happy. They had a bible study and both taught Sunday school.

One day Daphne said she wasn't feeling well. She had always been so active, that the chief had Dr. Samuels and the new doctor check her. They met and Samuels said, "We think she has cancer, Doctor Lee. We'll give her some medicine for her pain, but that's just to ease her. We will know soon if it is cancer."

It was, and it was a fast moving cancer. She was dead in three weeks. It was a sad time as everyone knew how the chief loved her. They had been so happy together.

The chief told Dr. Samuels that he needed some time off. Doctor Samuels said, "Take all the time you want."

He went to Winston and said, "I need a thousand dollars. I want to go away. It may be months before I return."

Winston said, "You've got it. If you run low use this check book and write a check. You're very valuable to our company, and you need to go where you feel you can shoulder this burden."

The chief left on the train. He knew where he needed to go, and that was Miami to see Ben. He went the same route that Ben had told him about. He took the riverboat from Kansas City to New Orleans. From there he took a ship to Miami.

In Miami he found someone who knew Ben and went to his office. They had written Ben about Daphne's death, and he had considered going there before another letter told of the chief's leaving. Ben thought he may go back to one of the Sioux tribes.

However as Ben was locking the office he turned and there was the chief. They both clung to one another and cried. Ben had never seen the chief cry. They stayed embraced for a long time, then Ben said, "Come to the house with me."

When Amy saw him, she burst into tears and came into his arms. Ben cried again.

They sat and Amy made some coffee. The chief then said, "When she died she had a smile on her face. She said she would wait for me in heaven. I couldn't stand it. I knew I had to be with you Ben. I have never loved anyone like I do you. You are part of me."

"Do you want to go somewhere where we can be alone, maybe an Indian tribe for awhile."

The chief said, "I would like that. I've heard the Apaches were sent to Florida. I would like to visit them until this wound is healed some."

Amy nodded, and said, "I will go to the office and fill in for you. You must go, the chief needs you."

They left the next day and traveled to where the Apache's were incarcerated. They went to the prison where Geronimo was and visited with him and the others.

Geronimo said, "It is good that you traveled this far to see about us. Please have your friends write the government that they have lied to us again. They said that we could return after two years, but that was four years ago. We are just wasting away here. I should have fought to the end and died a warriors death."

"No, you were lead by the Great Spirit. You did right. Had you not come, all would have died. You did right, great warrior."

They left depressed. The chief said, "When the white man came, it was all over for the Indians. They will always be kept like children, and the white men in Washington will continue to lie to them. They even lie to their own people. The Great Spirit will punish them, though."

Ben said, "Let's go back to the plains and hunt. Let's live off the land like we used to."

The chief thought this would be good. The traveled back to Wyoming where the last of Sioux were. They found Red Cloud's tribe. He was living on land that he had bargained with. Both their hair was now long, and Ben had a beard and a mustache. They had good weapons and good horses. Red Cloud showed Ben how to ride his horse Indian style. They road into the reservation and talked to the Indian agent. They said, "We want to take a few of the braves and go hunting."

The Indian agent said, "I'm not supposed to, but they need to get out once in awhile to hunt. Promise me you will bring them back in a month."

"Ben said, "If it's within my power I will."

They left the next morning. Ben had bought horses for four men. They left and went to the Black Hills. The miners had left and the hunting was good. They were all happy and brought back a lot of deer meat for those in the reservation. Ben left the horses with the Sioux and they left.

Ben said, "Do you want to see California?"

The chief nodded and they went to San Francisco and saw the sights. While they were looking at the ocean, the chief said, "I need to get back to work, and you need to go home, Ben. I will be alright now. Our souls were together enough to lift the death burden. Daphne would want me to work, so I shall."

Within a month, Ben was home. Amy was really glad to see him. As they sat drinking a mint julep on the veranda, she said, "You really did the best thing. Is the chief alright now?"

"No, but he's back to work. He has had a lot of heartache in his life. However, I have never had a friend like him. We became closer than a brothers over the years. I was happy for him when he met Daphne. She loved him dearly, and they had a few good years together."

She said, "I want to get married now. Will you marry me?"

Ben said, "I could never be happy without you. Do you want a big wedding?"

"No, but mother will. Let's go to Savanna a let her have the time of her life."

The wedding was a gala affair. Ben estimated about a thousand or more were there. Amy's mother was in seventh heaven. Ben was standing by his father-in-law and said, "Mother is having the time of her life." He smiled and said, "I'm glad she is enjoying herself."

They went to New Orleans for their honeymoon.

Chapter 16

A RETURN TO DENVER

At Christmas one year Ben said, "Amy, I want to go see my partners in Denver. We haven't seen them in five years now."

"Has it been that long?" Amy asked.

They left two weeks into December. They went to New Orleans and stayed three days because of some shows that were playing. They then took the riverboat to Kansas City and stayed there two nights. Amy said, "It's just like a honeymoon."

On the train they were able to get a Pullman and they slept in a single bunk. Sleep was sparse as Amy didn't ever sleep too long."

They finally arrived in Denver. They stayed three days before going to Hank's and Amy's ranch west of Verdi. Everyone was glad to see them. Sheriff Roscoe was still in Verdi and the town was quiet.

They continued to the ranch the next day. Cary said, "They have a play in Green Valley that everyone is raving about. Let's all go. All six of them rode in Hank's new carriage. It was fun, because they had a driver and a footman, Eduardo's kin, of course.

They saw the play and it was outstanding, They were getting into the carriage when gunfire started. Hank was helping Amy into the coach when a bullet from a high powered rifle passed through Hank and into Amy. Both were dead before they hit the ground. Everyone else went to the ground then. Barney had his pistol in hand and began firing in the direction the bullet had come from. They heard horses galloping off and then everything was quiet.

Ben had Amy in his arms and Cary had Hank in her arms. They looked at each other. Neither cried. They just sat there rocking back and forth with the bodies in their arms.

Barney said, "Let's take them to Billards. He's the local mortician. There's nothing we can do for them now."

They followed Barney's instructions, and put them in the coach and drove to Billards. On the way home, no one talked. They were all stunned. Barney finally broke the silence by saying. I'll go into Green Valley tomorrow and find out what was going down. When they arrived home they all went to bed.

Ben had only been in his bed for about five minutes when he heard his door open and close again. Cary slipped in beside him and held him. They both cried for awhile with nothing being said. They clung together until they finally slept.

Ben woke and Cary was still hanging onto him. It was early and he whispered, "You need to go back to your room. Others would not understand." Cary kissed him on the cheek and left. Ben laid there trying to think why God had taken Amy away from him. He knew he must take her home to her folks.

He got up and was having some coffee when Barney came in. Barney said, "It will never be the same without, Hank. He was not only my brother, but also my closest friend. I think Cary will survive, but I don't know if I will."

Ben said, "I've got to take Amy back to her folks, Barney. They'll want to bury her."

Barney said, "That's a long haul, but I know you have to do it."

They had a service for Hank the next day, then Ben left with Amy in her coffin.

He went the fastest way he could. He arrived in Savanna a little over a week later. He hired a hearse and they drove up to the Mason's mansion. One of the servants called to Lon and he came out and saw Ben getting down from the hearse. He called to his wife and she came to the porch. Upon seeing the hearse and Ben, she fell to her knees and cried, "No Lord, you can't have our Amy!"

Lon lifted her up and said, "We must endure. Amy would want us to be brave. Ben came upon the porch and hugged his mother-in- law. They both cried.

Lon said, "Have the men take her into the dining room and set her coffin on the table. People will want to see her. Will she be presentable?"

"I think so, I had her embalmed. I'll check her before anyone sees her."

After the coffin was on the table, Ben viewed her. She was the prettiest he had ever seen her. She looked like she was just resting with her eyes shut. He stood there awhile and Lon came in.

He said, "My, I have never seen her so beautiful. Mother! Come in here." They then all looked at her for sometime.

The next day they took the coffin to their church and left the coffin open. Hundreds of people passed by and most of them crying so heard they shook. Lon was standing next to Ben and said, "She touched a lot of people."

Ben stayed three days. He boarded a train to go back, and had just sat down when Cary was beside him. Ben held her and began to cry so hard he shook. He finally said, "You always were there for me."

Cary said, "We will always be together, now. We shall never part."

"How did you get here?"

"Two days after you left, I told Barney I needed to be alone for awhile. He nodded and I left. I knew Amy lived in Savanna. I was at her service and was always near you. I stayed in a hotel not far from the mansion and knew every move you made. I need you more than you need me, Ben. I feel I can't live without you. I feel like I did when I was sitting on that porch all alone in the world. Then you came and sat beside me and put your arm around me. I felt more love at that moment than at anytime in my life. I just knew you were an angel, as I had just prayed for one and there you were. I remember asking if you were an angel and you said, 'No, but I was sent by one.' For a long time I felt you were an angel. I never felt as comfortable with anyone than I did you. You are my man now, until death us do part. The way everyone is dying, that may be soon.

"When daddy wrote and I saw him after two years, I wanted his hug more than anything in the world. I now feel that with you. I want your arms about me until I die."

Ben said, "I guess God had us as a couple before the world was made. We were born for each other Cary. We grew apart though."

"Yes. I will tell you why we did, but not today. We will have to be someplace that is right."

"Where might that be?"

"I don't know, but we'll find it. It's summer, let's go to Canada. Maybe Nova Scotia or Newfoundland."

"Sounds great to me."

"It maybe sometime before we make love, but I know we will. I want your babies. I don't know why, but I didn't want any children when I was married to Hank, and I think he felt the same way. There was always too much to do. I know you are well to do, but Ben, I'm a millionaire. My dad and his partner mined one of the richest gold mines in the world. Then Barney and Hank mined it, and there is still plenty of gold. I took the money dad had, and put it into stocks that made me ten times their value. I now have all the money out of the market and am just drawing interest on it. So, Mr. Lee, you are rich as we are now married. Mr. and Mrs. Lee."

"I don't know if I could have gotten through this without you, Cary. You seem to give me the best medicine in the world, pure love."

She then cuddled up with him. She said, "I rented a Pullman so I can hold you all night."

They went to Nova Scotia and stayed in Halifax. They ate sea food and loved the setting. They then traveled to St. Johns in Newfoundland and loved it there although it was just a fishing village. The smell finally drove them away.

They caught a ship going to London, with stops in Iceland and the Faroe Islands. They were finally in a suite at a Grand Hotel in London.

They were sitting on a balcony drinking a gin and tonic when Cary suddenly said, "I will now tell you why we pulled apart.

"I witnessed Odom and his five men kill dad. Each one of them fired into him. He had just told Odom he would sell out to him for a very low price. Odom said, 'It can't be as cheap as a bullet.'

"I hid in a closet with clothes piled all over me. After they left, I swore I would kill them. You remember those knockout drops, Mr. Baker used on Robert?" Ben nodded.

"Well I stole them and replaced them with a bottle I bought, and filled it with water. I owned a donut shop and one night two of Odom's hands were riding home. I stopped them and asked if they wanted a donut and coffee before they rode home. I had knockout drops in their coffee. I took them in my buggy to the Odom's ranch and used their ropes and horses to pull them up and hanged them.

"Three months later I did the same with two more of Odom's hands.

"Odom's foreman then decided to leave, and I was lucky to see him riding out late one night. I used the drops on him and hung him.

"Odom then wanted to sell out, I read the ad in the paper and rode out the next day. I made him an offer of twelve thousand in cash and put the money on the table.

"While he was signing the deed to his place and cattle over to me, I made coffee. When he awoke his hands were tied behind his back and he was being held up by a rope under his armpits while standing on my buggy. He had a hangman's noose around his neck. I cut the rope holding him up, which left him standing with just the noose around his neck. I waited until he was completely lucid and told him how I watched him kill my daddy. I asked him if he had any last words. All he could say was 'Please don't hang me.'

"I then got into my buggy and drove off.

"I buried him where he had buried his crew, my daddy and his partner.

"It changed me. I was harder and much more worldly. I didn't think I was good enough for you then. I wanted you to leave me for your own good, and you did.

"I married Hank, but I never loved him like I did you. I needed sex and he gave that to me. What do you think of me now?"

"You won't believe this. I told Amy our complete story and how we had grown apart. I said you had changed after you became a woman. She sat a minute or two and then said that you changed because of something that either happened to you or you did. She said you still loved me. She said I hadn't changed, it was all you.

"I didn't believe her, but she was right. She even knew who killed her first husband. I finally found that out, too, and he's serving thirty years.

"She was right, you never stopped loving me. You did what you did because you loved me. That alone tells me we should be together forever."

"Will you make love to me tonight?"

"Yes. I feel we are married, now, and always will be. We don't have to have a ceremony to be married. Only God can sanctify a marriage and he's done that."

When they were in bed, Cary said, "Holding you is the best part of my life. I loved you the day you put your arm around me on that porch. I can't describe the love you poured over me. I think it will be the same when Jesus takes us in his arms, when we go home. He just gave me a look at what love can be. I want to be as close to you as I can be and that will be when we are of one flesh. I will then feel like I am close as I can be to you. Our souls shall intertwine and we will become one."

They kissed and held each other a long time before they became one. Ben thought, "*I think Cary was the one God wanted me to have, he gave me Amy to learn that. She taught me a lot. That woman was a good teacher.*"

Everywhere they went, Cary clung to Ben. He liked it. He felt warmer and knew he was loved the fullest anyone on earth could love him.

***

The chief was treating a woman in the clinic for pain in her elbow. She had been in several times and when the chief was not available, she would just say, I will wait. He knows my body.

Doctor Samuels was at the receptionist's desk, when the woman said she would wait. he smiled to himself and thought, "*That woman has a thing for Dr. Lee.*"

At the end of the day, the three doctors always sat together and went over the happenings of the day.

Doctor Samuels said, "I think Mrs. Crawford has a thing for you Doctor Lee."

The chief was astounded. He said, "I think she is just grateful as I have helped her through some pain that was severe."

"No, the other doctor said, "I noticed how she looked at you, and thought the same thing."

"Well, some of our patients confuse gratitude with love sometimes," the chief said.

"Not in this case," Doctor Samuels said. "I think she loves you. Although mature, she is still comely."

"What are you getting at, Doctor Samuels?"

"I think you owe it to her to treat the love symptom outside the clinic. Don't you Bill?"

"Absolutely. I think you would be remiss in your responsibility if you just left her hanging."

The chief didn't realize the humor of the two, and thought they were serious. He then said, "What should I do?"

"Ask her to go with you to that play at the Cow Palace tomorrow. I've seen it, and it's really good. You both would enjoy it and you would be doing your duty at the same time."

The chiefs brow knitted as he thought. He then said, "How would I go about that?"

"Send a messenger inviting her to go with you and tell her a time you will pick her up. Have a messenger wait for a reply."

The chief was apprehensive, but he thought they were serious about treating the woman outside the clinic. He then said, "I'll do it. If she turns me down, then nothing is lost."

Mrs. Crawford was delightfully surprised. She wrote, "I will be ready at six-thirty."

The chief came in one of the Lee's carriages with a driver and footman. Mrs. Crawford was delighted. She had worn a beautiful gown and the chief was dressed in a dark suit and white shirt with a back bow tie.

As they drove, Mrs. Crawford said, "I have wanted to see you outside the office for sometime, Doctor Lee, however, I didn't know how to go about it without embarrassing us both. I'm delighted to be with you."

The chief said, "You are very beautiful, Mrs. Crawford. That gown becomes you."

"Call me Kathryn. May I call you by your first name?"

"I don't have a first name in English. You see I'm an Indian and I have never had a first name. Why don't you give me one."

Kathryn was astounded. She said, "What a privilege, Doctor Lee. I will have to think about this awhile, but I surely want to do this."

They were silent awhile and as they drove, she said, "It must be a name that honors you, as you are someone special. Are you really an Indian, Doctor Lee?"

He smiled and said, "Yes I am. I have a long story which I hope to relate to you in the future. Tonight we should just enjoy being with one another."

If Kathryn wasn't in love before, she was now. She looked at him with such tenderness, the chief was somewhat smitten.

She could tell his look and said, "Do you feel it, Doctor Lee?"

"Feel what, Kathryn?"

"The magic that has passed between us."

"You mean like love?"

"Yes, if you would, love. I have more than liked you for sometime, but thought you wouldn't want a woman as old as me."

"Why not, you are vibrant and beautiful, so much so I do feel love."

"Please kiss me then," and she leaned toward him with her eyes closed.

The chief knew he had to kiss her, so he did. When he did she put her arms around his neck and said, "I have wanted you to do this for a long time. I love you."

The chief was speechless, so he just held her very tightly and then kissed her again.

They became a couple then. The chief was very comfortable with her. When the chief loved someone it was not superficial, but profound.

He prayed many times for her and their relationship. They were married six months later. By then he had told her his life story and especially about Ben.

Kathryn said, "You really love Ben don't you?"

"Yes, but I feel lost without him. He has been gone for two years now and no one knows where he is. I wrote his wife's folks in Savanna, and they hadn't heard from him either. I know Ben would not take his life. He is just making a new life."

He then said, "Funny, Cary left two days after Ben left with his wife's coffin. She too has been gone for two years. Do you suppose they're together?"

After you told me how they met, and the love that passed between them, that is a sure thing."

The chief had never thought of that. He thought, *They did have a strong love, almost a holy love.* He smiled then and said aloud, "Yes, they are together."

Kathryn smiled and said, "I agree."

"By the way, I have thought of your name. It is a Biblical name. I chose it because to me St. Paul was the greatest of the disciples of Christ. I shall name you, Paul."

"Thank you Kathryn. I like the name, Paul Lee." He laughed then and said, "It surely beat's 'Chief,'" and they both laughed.

He then said, "Of course my friends have called me, 'Chief.' for so long it will be hard for them. I don't mind them calling me 'Chief.' In fact I took it as an honor."

"Well, my friends will now call you Paul. Do you mind living in my house, Paul?"

"No. We could have lived at the hotel, but you are more comfortable in your own home."

Chapter 17 =================

THE HOMECOMING

Cary and Ben lived in London for three weeks, then moved to Paris. They loved Paris so much they took French lessons and learned to speak it. They now only talked French to each other.

Cary hired a linguist to weed out their accent. They knew this would take sometime. There was always something to do there. They rented a flat in the busiest part of Paris and enjoyed eating at the sidewalk cafes. The wine was excellent. They both became coinsures of wine. They met several couples who they both thought eccentric, but fun to be with.

They both were now interested in art as one of their friends was an artist. He schooled them on art. They took him to many art galleries. Cary bought several paintings. One was huge.

Ben said, "How are we going to fit that in our flat?"

"We're not. I'm sending it home. I want to buy at least ten painting and send them home to our mansion. I will instruct Debbie to hang them. She's good at that. We must eventually go home you know."

"Yes, we have been gone so long, I'm sure everyone has figured out we are together."

"You're right, they will know, but I don't care. They all know how we love one another."

They went to Italy and visited Venice, Milan, Pisa, Rome, Naples and Capri. While there Cary bought seven tapestries. One was huge and she paid two thousand dollars for it. She had them all shipped to the mansion.

When the paintings and tapestries began showing up at the mansion, Debbie was delighted. She loved hanging them. She sat and drew out the different rooms, then decided what went where. Barney just marveled at them. He said, "Cary has a great eye for art, but you have know just where to put them. I would never figure that out."

They came back through Switzerland and visited their art galleries. When they returned to Paris, Cary said, "It is time to go home,"

"What made you decide that?" Ben asked.

"Because I am pregnant."

Ben was stunned. He came to her and held her. He then began to cry and she held him tightly and cried with him.

He finally said, "This is the happiest day of my life."

"Me too. I found out in Switzerland, but wanted to make sure before I told you. I thought I was barren, but here we are with another Lee. What sex would you prefer, Ben?"

"I don't care, just so it's healthy. I just hope there are more to come. I would like to fill that mansion so full Barney and Debbie would feel crowded."

"They might have some kids, too, by now."

"I hope so. The children will feel like brothers and sisters rather than cousins. Do you want to have the baby here and wait to go home?"

Cary said, "Of course not. If it is a boy he must be born in America to be president."

Ben laughed and said, "You have some high expectations. Remember he comes from two orphans."

"Yes, we have come far from the two people standing in that stream stark naked and me with sores all over my body. That always amazed me how tender you were when you treated each spot. Oh, the love I had for you. I wanted to make love to you as soon as I could. I thought giving you love like that, would make you love me."

"It would have, but I knew it wasn't right. However, we might have had eight children by now."

They arrived in Verdi and Cary's stomach was sticking out so everyone could see she was pregnant. Cary was proud carrying Ben's baby. She first went to the donut shop with Ben. Mildred shouted, "Your pregnant, Cary! How wonderful. I'm leaving to get Cole, he's home." With that she tore out the back door and was gone. Greta came and hugged her. She then looked at Ben and said, "I suppose you're the proud father?"

Ben smiled and said, "I'm Ben Lee. We met briefly some years ago. I was with my first wife, Amy."

"Oh yes, I was so taken with her beauty, that I probably didn't notice you so much. I have never seen a woman that beautiful. What a pity for her to be taken so soon. Everyone I know says she was the most beautiful woman in the world. Eduardo and Rudi think she was an angel, and maybe she was.

"However, I'm glad you found Cary. She may not be as pretty as your first wife, but she is prettier inside that anyone I know."

'Thank you Greta."

About that time the mayor and sheriff came in. The mayor saw Cary and ran to her. He embraced her, then noticed she was pregnant. He said, "You can't know how people grieved for you. Verdi was not the same without Hank and you.

"Is this your new husband?"

"Yes, this is Ben Lee. You may remember his wife who was killed when Hank was."

"Oh, lord, what a tragic day. That was the most beautiful woman anyone had ever seen. I'm glad you two got together. Where have you been?"

"Paris mostly." Before the mayor could comment, Cole burst into the café and embraced Cary. He said, Partner, I was lost without you. Even Mildred said I was moping about."

Mildred said, "He lost his best friend, and it was hard to cheer him up. He told me everyday that he needed you here to help him make decisions. Well, he muddled through and has built a really good construction company."

They left and went to the mansion. They stopped and visited Rudi and Juanita before they went to the mansion. Juanita insisted that they eat with them as she was just putting dinner on the table. They stayed and enjoyed their company. Their two boys were men now, and were also glad to see them.

As they were driving up to the Mansion, Barney was just coming out the door. He turned and yelled, "Debbie come quick the prodigal daughter has returned."

Debbie came running and got to Cary before Barney. They hugged while Barney was shaking Ben's hand.

Barney said, "After a year, everyone just knew you had found each other. I felt it after you had been gone a month. I remembered how you loved one another and thought that God had a hand in that."

"You were right, Barney. God brought us together, and now we have something to show for it."

Barney said, "I can see. We have a two year old girl and Debbie is pregnant again. I hope you and I can fill up this place, Ben."

Ben laughed and said, "I'll try to do my part."

The next day they went to the south ranch to see Eduardo and Maria. Upon seeing them, Eduardo ran to the house and yelled for Maria to come. Maria was afraid something bad had happened and came quickly. When she saw Cary, she feel to her knees and said, "Thank you, Lord."

She then rose and went to Cary and hugged her. Eduardo had left to get his sons who were in the barn.

The old Odom place had changed much. Eduardo and his boys had built a huge barn and there were two houses that were built.

As Cary was looking at the new construction, Maria said, "Both our boys are now married and needed their own homes."

The boys and their wives came up and the wives were introduced. Before they went to the house, Eduardo said, "We created a monument for your first wife, Ben. Would you like to see it?"

They were shown to the gravesite and there was a statue of the Virgin and on the caption it read: An angel came here to see us, then was taken by God. Such beauty has never been know on this earth. We praise you, Lord for letting her be with us. Amen.

Ben put his arm around Eduardo and said, "Thank you, Eduardo, she was an angel."

They left after they had visited and had some cool drinks that Juanita made. Everyone hugged Cary before she left.

When they were back at the mansion, Debbie said, "I never had such a good time as hanging those paintings and tapestries. Please change their positions if you don't like the arrangements."

Cary said, "I wouldn't change a thing. You are an artist yourself, knowing just where to hang each. I adore where they are."

Barney said, "This house looks like a museum. I love it. No wonder you were gone for years. It took that much time to pick the paintings and tapestries out. I need to know about all of them as when people ask, I don't want to look like the dumb cowboy I am."

Both Ben and Cary told them about the paintings and tapestries. They had even bought books that were in English that told of the French Impressionist and some of the other art. Both Barney and Debbie were interested.

The baby came in November and it was a little girl. They named her Amy after Ben's first wife. When Eduardo and Juanita came to see the baby and learned its name they both crossed themselves and went to one knee briefly.

Cary said, "Eduardo, you and Juanita with be her godparents."

Eduardo said, "What a privilege. He turned to Juanita, who had tears in her eyes, and said, "We will look after her throughout her life."

After they had gone, Ben said, "That was a wonderful gesture, Cary, but then again that's you."

Ben did not work into the work force of the ranch, instead he tended to the stocks and bonds with Cary's help. They loved the financial end and discussed each transaction they made. They had a telegraph line constructed to the mansion. There they could trade stock at their leisure.

Ben said, "Come spring I want to go back to Savanna and show Lon and Lara our baby and that we named her after their Amy."

Cary said, "After that, I want to go back to Paris, before we forget the language."

They did just that. In Savanna they told their life stories to Lara and Lon.

Lon said, "I'm glad you found each other. I've thought a lot about Amy. She had a good life. She loved you more than she did Roger. Both of us knew that. You were good to her."

Lon told how he had sold the business, but not the house. He said, "We kept it as we like to go down there some. You can stay there anytime you want. You can live there if you want to."

They went to the cemetery and visited Amy's grave. While there Ben told how she was thought of as an Angel in Verdi. He told of the monument and the inscription. He said, "Everywhere she went, she brought sunlight to those around her."

Lon said, "You will never know how grateful we are that you came. Promise us you will write and if possible send us pictures of Amy as she grows up. We will think of her as our granddaughter."

He then turned to Cary and said, "I am so grateful that you were there for Ben. It warms our heart that he's happy."

In Paris, they were able to rent the same flat that they had rented before. Many people didn't even know they had left and life went on as usual.

Cary said, "I would like to see Germany, Holland, and maybe Denmark."

They made arrangements and saw them all, and included Belgium. They were gone eight month, then returned to Paris.

Amy was now starting to walk and say things. They loved it. Cary said, "I'm pregnant again. So let's time it so we will be in Verdi three months before the child is due.

It worked well and Cary was again large when they came to Verdi. During her last weeks they went in to Denver to a hospital to have the baby. It was another girl. Ben said, "I'm happy that she is a girl. A girl needs a sister. If we have a boy the next time, they will mother him."

They named the girl, Alta, not necessarily for Alta Dobbs, but they just liked the name.

When Alta turned one, they went back to Paris. Ben said, "You are the most fertile in Paris."

"That's because we make love more often there. The atmosphere is more conducive to love," said Cary.

They didn't rent their old flat as it was now too small for them. Ben said, "Let's buy an apartment. One that we really like and will use. Other people can use it, also. I would like Barney to take Debbie here."

"Even Cole and Mildred could come," said Cary.

They searched most days until they came to a place overlooking the Seine. It had a wonderful view and was in an upscale building that had a guard on duty in the lobby twenty-four hours a day. It was a bit pricey, but Cary wanted it, so they bought it.

They lived there two years before coming home. They always stopped by to see Ben's in-laws in Savanna as they both knew that they would want to see Amy.

When they reached home they decided to have a party and invited all their friends.

Barney said, "I hope you will stay home for awhile. It's lonely when you're gone.

Cary said, "We will stay for awhile, but we love Paris. I'm hoping you and Debbie will come. We have room for you. Although you will be in one room. It's quite large, though."

Life settled down to normal at the mansion west of Verdi, and they continued having parties every Saturday night unless a drama or some other show was playing in Green Valley.

Both families had three children and were very happy.

The End

Printed in the United States
By Bookmasters